# The Maids Tragedy

Francis Beaumont and John Fletcher

## Persons Represented in the Play.

King.

Lysippus, *brother to the King.*

Amintor, *a Noble Gentleman.*

Evadne, *Wife to* Amintor.

Malantius}
Diphilius } *Brothers to* Evadne.

Aspatia, *troth-plight wife to* Amnitor.

Calianax, *an old humorous Lord, and
Father to* Aspatia.

Cleon      }
Strato     } *Gentlemen.*

Diagoras, *a Servant.*

Antiphila }
Olympias} *waiting Gentlewomen to* Aspatia.

Dula, *a Lady.*

Night      }
Cynthia   }
Neptune  }
Eolus      } *Maskers.*

# The Maids Tragedy

*Actus primus. Scena prima.*

Enter *Cleon, Strato, Lysippus, Diphilus.*

*Cleon.*  The rest are making ready Sir.

*Strat.*  So let them, there's time enough.

*Diph.*  You are the brother to the King, my Lord, we'll take your word.

*Lys.*  *Strato*, thou hast some skill in Poetry, What thinkst thou of a Mask? will it be well?

*Strat.*  As well as Mask can be.

*Lys.*  As Mask can be?

*Strat.*  Yes, they must commend their King, and speak in praise of the Assembly, bless the Bride and Bridegroom, in person of some God; th'are tyed to rules of flattery.

*Cle.*  See, good my Lord, who is return'd!

*Lys.*  Noble *Melantius!*

[*Enter Melantius.*

The Land by me welcomes thy vertues home to *Rhodes*, thou that with blood abroad buyest us our peace; the breath of King is like the breath of Gods; My brother wisht thee here, and thou art here; he will be too kind, and weary thee with often welcomes; but the time doth give thee a welcome above this or all the worlds.

*Mel.*  My Lord, my thanks; but these scratcht limbs of mine have spoke my love and truth unto my friends, more than my tongue ere could: my mind's the same it ever was to you; where I find worth, I love the keeper, till he let it go, And then I follow it.

*Diph.*  Hail worthy brother!

1

He that rejoyces not at your return
In safety, is mine enemy for ever.

Mel.    I thank thee *Diphilus*: but thou art faulty;
I sent for thee to exercise thine armes
With me at *Patria*: thou cam'st not *Diphilus*: 'Twas  ill.

Diph.    My noble brother, my excuse
Is my King's strict command, which you my Lord
Can witness with me.

Lys.    'Tis true *Melantius*,
He might not come till the solemnity
Of this great match were past.

Diph.    Have you heard of it?

Mel.    Yes, I have given cause to those that
Envy my deeds abroad, to call me gamesome;
I have no other business here at *Rhodes*.

Lys.    We have a Mask to night,
And you must tread a Soldiers measure.

Mel.    These soft and silken wars are not for me;
The Musick must be shrill, and all confus'd,
That stirs my blood, and then I dance with armes:
But is *Amintor* Wed?

Diph.    This day.

Mel.    All joyes upon him, for he is my friend:
Wonder not that I call a man so young my friend,
His worth is great; valiant he is, and temperate,
And one that never thinks his life his own,
If his friend need it: when he was a boy,
As oft as I return'd (as without boast)
I brought home conquest, he would gaze upon me,
And view me round, to find in what one limb
The vertue lay to do those things he heard:
Then would he wish to see my Sword, and feel
The quickness of the edge, and in his hand
Weigh it; he oft would make me smile at this;

His youth did promise much, and his ripe years
Will see it all perform'd.

[*Enter Aspatia, passing by.*

*Melan.* Hail Maid and Wife!
Thou fair *Aspatia*, may the holy knot
That thou hast tyed to day, last till the hand
Of age undo't; may'st thou bring a race
Unto *Amintor* that may fill the world
Successively with Souldiers.

*Asp.* My hard fortunes
Deserve not scorn; for I was never proud
When they were good.

[*Exit Aspatia.*

*Mel.* How's this?

*Lys.* You are mistaken, for she is not married.

*Mel.* You said *Amintor* was.

*Diph.* 'Tis true; but

*Mel.* Pardon me, I did receive
Letters at *Patria*, from my *Amintor*,
That he should marry her.

*Diph.* And so it stood,
In all opinion long; but your arrival
Made me imagine you had heard the change.

*Mel.* Who hath he taken then?

*Lys.* A Lady Sir,
That bears the light above her, and strikes dead
With flashes of her eye; the fair *Evadne* your
vertuous Sister.

*Mel.* Peace of heart betwixt them: but this is strange.

*Lys.*  The King my brother did it
　　　　To honour you; and these solemnities
　　　　Are at his charge.

*Mel.*  'Tis Royal, like himself;
　　　　But I am sad, my speech bears so unfortunate a sound
　　　　To beautiful *Aspatia*; there is rage
　　　　Hid in her fathers breast; *Calianax*
　　　　Bent long against me, and he should not think,
　　　　If I could call it back, that I would take
　　　　So base revenges, as to scorn the state
　　　　Of his neglected daughter: holds he still his greatness with
　　　　the King?

*Lys.*  Yes; but this Lady
　　　　Walks discontented, with her watry eyes
　　　　Bent on the earth: the unfrequented woods
　　　　Are her delight; and when she sees a bank
　　　　Stuck full of flowers, she with a sigh will tell
　　　　Her servants what a pretty place it were
　　　　To bury lovers in, and make her maids
　　　　Pluck'em, and strow her over like a Corse.
　　　　She carries with her an infectious grief
　　　　That strikes all her beholders, she will sing
　　　　The mournful'st things that ever ear hath heard,
　　　　And sigh, and sing again, and when the rest
　　　　Of our young Ladies in their wanton blood,
　　　　Tell mirthful tales in course that fill the room
　　　　With laughter, she will with so sad a look
　　　　Bring forth a story of the silent death
　　　　Of some forsaken Virgin, which her grief
　　　　Will put in such a phrase, that ere she end,
　　　　She'l send them weeping one by one away.

*Mel.*  She has a brother under my command
　　　　Like her, a face as womanish as hers,
　　　　But with a spirit that hath much out-grown
　　　　The number of his years.

　　　　　　　　　　[*Enter Amintor.*

*Cle.*  My Lord the Bridegroom!

# The Maids Tragedy

*Mel.*     I might run fiercely, not more hastily
        Upon my foe: I love thee well *Amintor*,
        My mouth is much too narrow for my heart;
        I joy to look upon those eyes of thine;
        Thou art my friend, but my disorder'd speech cuts off
        my love.

*Amin.*    Thou art *Melantius*;
        All love is spoke in that, a sacrifice
        To thank the gods, *Melantius* is return'd
        In safety; victory sits on his sword
        As she was wont; may she build there and dwell,
        And may thy Armour be as it hath been,
        Only thy valour and thy innocence.
        What endless treasures would our enemies give,
        That I might hold thee still thus!

*Mel.*     I am but poor in words, but credit me young man,
        Thy Mother could no more but weep, for joy to see thee
        After long absence; all the wounds I have,
        Fetch not so much away, nor all the cryes
        Of Widowed Mothers: but this is peace;
        And what was War?

*Amin.*    Pardon thou holy God
        Of Marriage bed, and frown not, I am forc't
        In answer of such noble tears as those,
        To weep upon my Wedding day.

*Mel.*     I fear thou art grown too sick; for I hear
        A Lady mourns for thee, men say to death,
        Forsaken of thee, on what terms I know not.

*Amin.*    She had my promise, but the King forbad it,
        And made me make this worthy change, thy Sister
        Accompanied with graces above her,
        With whom I long to lose my lusty youth,
        And grow old in her arms.

*Mel.*     Be prosperous.

*[Enter Messenger.*

5

*Messen.* My Lord, the Maskers rage for you.

*Lys.* We are gone. *Cleon, Strata, Diphilus.*

*Amin.* Wee'l all attend you, we shall trouble you
With our solemnities.

*Mel.* Not so *Amintor.*
But if you laugh at my rude carriage
In peace, I'le do as much for you in War
When you come thither: yet I have a Mistress
To bring to your delights; rough though I am,
I have a Mistress, and she has a heart,
She saies, but trust me, it is stone, no better,
There is no place that I can challenge in't.
But you stand still, and here my way lies.

[*Exit.*

*Enter Calianax with Diagoras.*

*Cal.* *Diagoras,* look to the doors better for shame, you let in all the world, and anon the King will rail at me; why very well said, by *Jove* the King will have the show i'th' Court.

*Diag.* Why do you swear so my Lord?
You know he'l have it here.

*Cal.* By this light if he be wise he will not.

*Diag.* And if he will not be wise, you are forsworn.

*Cal.* One may wear his heart out with swearing, and get thanks on no side, I'le be gone, look to't who will.

*Diag.* My Lord, I will never keep them out.
Pray stay, your looks will terrifie them.

*Cal.* My looks terrifie them, you Coxcombly Ass you! I'le be judg'd by all the company whether thou hast not a worse face than I—

*Diag.* I mean, because they know you and your Office.

6

Cal.      Office! I would I could put it off, I am sure I sweat quite through my Office, I might have made room at my Daughters Wedding, they had near kill'd her among them. And now I must do service for him that hath forsaken her; serve that will.

*[Exit Calianax.*

Diag.     IIe's so humourous since his daughter was forsaken: hark, hark, there, there, so, so, codes, codes.
       What now?

*[Within. knock within.*

Mel.     Open the door.

Diag.     Who's there?

Mel.     Melantius.

Diag.     I hope your Lordship brings no troop with you, for if you do, I must return them.

*[Enter Melantius.*

Mel.     None but this Lady Sir.

*[And a Lady.*

Diag.     The Ladies are all plac'd above, save those that come in the Kings Troop, the best of *Rhodes* sit there, and there's room.

Mel.     I thank you Sir: when I have seen you plac'd
      Madam, I must attend the King; but the Mask done, I'le
      wait on you again.

Diag.  Stand back there, room for my Lord *Melantius*, pray bear back, this is no place for such youths and their Truls, let the doors shut agen; I, do your heads itch? I'le scratch them for you: so now thrust and hang: again, who is't now? I cannot blame my Lord *Calianax* for going away; would he were here, he would run raging among them, and break a dozen wiser heads than his own in the twinkling of an eye: what's the news now?

*[Within.*

I pray can you help me to the speech of the Master Cook?

*Diag.*  If I open the door I'le cook some of your Calvesheads.
Peace Rogues.—again,—who is't?

*Mel.*  *Melantius within. Enter Calianax to Melantius.*

*Cal.*  Let him not in.

*Diag.*  O my Lord I must; make room there for my
Lord; is your Lady plac't?

*Mel.*  Yes Sir, I thank you my Lord *Calianax*: well met,
Your causless hate to me I hope is buried.

*Cal.*  Yes, I do service for your Sister here,
That brings my own poor Child to timeless death;
She loves your friend *Amintor*, such another false-hearted
Lord as you.

*Mel.*  You do me wrong,
A most unmanly one, and I am slow
In taking vengeance, but be well advis'd.

*Cal.*  It may be so: who placed the Lady there so near the
presence of the King?

*Mel.*  I did.

*Cal.*  My Lord she must not sit there.

*Mel.*  Why?

*Cal.*  The place is kept for women of more worth.
*Mel.*  More worth than she? it mis-becomes your Age
And place to be thus womanish; forbear;
What you have spoke, I am content to think
The Palsey shook your tongue to.

*Cal.*  Why 'tis well if I stand here to place mens wenches.

*Mel.*  I shall forget this place, thy Age, my safety, and through all,
  cut that poor sickly week thou hast to live, away from
  thee.

*Cal.*  Nay, I know you can fight for your Whore.

*Mel.*  Bate the King, and be he flesh and blood,
  He lyes that saies it, thy mother at fifteen
  Was black and sinful to her.

*Diag.*  Good my Lord!

*Mel.*  Some god pluck threescore years from that fond man,
  That I may kill him, and not stain mine honour;
  It is the curse of Souldiers, that in peace
  They shall be brain'd by such ignoble men,
  As (if the Land were troubled) would with tears
  And knees beg succour from 'em: would that blood
  (That sea of blood) that I have lost in fight,
  Were running in thy veins, that it might make thee
  Apt to say less, or able to maintain,
  Shouldst thou say more, — This *Rhodes* I see is nought
  But a place priviledg'd to do men wrong.

*Cal.*  I, you may say your pleasure.

[*Enter Amintor.*

*Amint.*  What vilde injury
  Has stirr'd my worthy friend, who is as slow
  To fight with words, as he is quick of hand?

*Mel.*  That heap of age which I should reverence
  If it were temperate: but testy years
  Are most contemptible.

*Amint.*  Good Sir forbear.

*Cal.*  There is just such another as your self.

*Amint.*  He will wrong you, or me, or any man,
  And talk as if he had no life to lose
  Since this our match: the King is coming in,

9

> I would not for more wealth than I enjoy,
> He should perceive you raging, he did hear
> You were at difference now, which hastned him.

*Cal.*    Make room there.

*Hoboyes play within.*

*Enter King, Evadne, Aspatia, Lords and Ladies.*

*King.*    Melantius, thou art welcome, and my love
     Is with thee still; but this is not a place
     To brabble in; *Calianax,* joyn hands.

*Cal.*    He shall not have my hand.

*King.*    This is no time
     To force you to't, I do love you both:
     *Calianax,* you look well to your Office;
     And you *Melantius* are welcome home; begin the Mask.

*Mel.*    Sister, I joy to see you, and your choice,
     You lookt with my eyes when you took that man;
     Be happy in him.

                             [*Recorders.*

*Evad.*    O my dearest brother!
     Your presence is more joyful than this day can be unto me.

*The Mask.*

*Night rises in mists.*

*Nigh.*    Our raign is come; for in the raging Sea
     The Sun is drown'd, and with him fell the day:
     Bright *Cinthia* hear my voice, I am the Night
     For whom thou bear'st about thy borrowed light;
     Appear, no longer thy pale visage shrowd,
     But strike thy silver horn through a cloud,
     And send a beam upon my swarthy face,
     By which I may discover all the place
     And persons, and how many longing eyes

# The Maids Tragedy

Are come to wait on our solemnities.

*[Enter Cinthia.*

How dull and black am I! I could not find
This beauty without thee, I am so blind;
Methinks they shew like to those Eastern streaks
That warn us hence before the morning breaks;
Back my pale servant, for these eyes know how
To shoot far more and quicker rayes than thou.

*Cinth.* Great Queen, they be a Troop for whom alone
One of my clearest moons I have put on;
A Troop that looks as if thy self and I
Had pluckt our rains in, and our whips laid by
To gaze upon these Mortals, that appear
Brighter than we.

*Night.* Then let us keep 'em here,
And never more our Chariots drive away,
But hold our places, and out-shine the day.

*Cinth.* Great Queen of shadows, you are pleas'd to speak
Of more than may be done; we may not break
The gods decrees, but when our time is come,
Must drive away and give the day our room.
Yet whil'st our raign lasts, let us stretch our power
To give our servants one contented hour,
With such unwonted solemn grace and state,
As may for ever after force them hate
Our brothers glorious beams, and wish the night
Crown'd with a thousand stars, and our cold light:
For almost all the world their service bend
To *Phoebus* and in vain my light I lend,
Gaz'd on unto my setting from my rise
Almost of none, but of unquiet eyes.

*Nigh.* Then shine at full, fair Queen, and by thy power
Produce a birth to crown this happy hour;
Of Nymphs and Shepherds let their songs discover,
Easie and sweet, who is a happy Lover;
Or if thou woot, then call thine own *Endymion*
From the sweet flowry bed he lies upon,

On *Latmus* top, thy pale beams drawn away,
And of this long night let him make a day.

*Cinth.*   Thou dream'st dark Queen, that fair boy was not mine,
         Nor went I down to kiss him; ease and wine
         Have bred these bold tales; Poets when they rage,
         Turn gods to men, and make an hour an age;
         But I will give a greater state and glory,
         And raise to time a noble memory
         Of what these Lovers are; rise, rise, I say,
         Thou power of deeps, thy surges laid away,
         *Neptune* great King of waters, and by me
         Be proud to be commanded.

                     [Neptune rises.

*Nep.*   *Cinthia*, see,
         Thy word hath fetcht me hither, let me know why I
         ascend.

*Cinth.*   Doth this majestick show
         Give thee no knowledge yet?

*Nep.*   Yes, now I see.
         Something intended *(Cinthia)* worthy thee;
         Go on, I'le be a helper.

*Cinth.*   Hie thee then,
         And charge the wind flie from his Rockie Den.
         Let loose thy subjects, only *Boreas*
         Too foul for our intention as he was;
         Still keep him fast chain'd; we must have none here
         But vernal blasts, and gentle winds appear,
         Such as blow flowers, and through the glad Boughs sing
         Many soft welcomes to the lusty spring.
         These are our musick: next, thy watry race
         Bring on in couples; we are pleas'd to grace
         This noble night, each in their richest things
         Your own deeps or the broken vessel brings;
         Be prodigal, and I shall be as kind,
         And shine at full upon you.

*Nep.*   Ho the wind

The Maids Tragedy

Commanding *Eolus!*

[Enter Eolus out of a Rock.

*Eol.*  Great *Neptune!*

*Nep.*  He.

*Eol.*  What is thy will?

*Nep.*  We do command thee free
         *Favonius* and thy milder winds to wait
         Upon our *Cinthia*, but tye *Boreas* straight;
         He's too rebellious.

*Eol.*  I shall do it.

*Nep.*  Do, great master of the flood, and all below,
         Thy full command has taken.

*Eol.*  Ho! the main;
         *Neptune.*

*Nep.*  Here.

*Eol.*  *Boreas* has broke his chain,
         And struggling with the rest, has got away.

*Nep.*  Let him alone, I'le take him up at sea;
         He will not long be thence; go once again
         And call out of the bottoms of the Main,
         Blew *Proteus*, and the rest; charge them put on
         Their greatest pearls, and the most sparkling stone
         The bearing Rock breeds, till this night is done
         By me a solemn honour to the Moon;
         Flie like a full sail.

*Eol.*  I am gone.

*Cin.*  Dark night,
         Strike a full silence, do a thorow right
         To this great *Chorus*, that our Musick may
         Touch high as heaven, and make the East break day

13

The Maids Tragedy

At mid-[n]ight.

[*Musick.*

SONG.

Cinthia *to thy power, and them we obey.*
*Joy to this great company, and no day*
*Come to steal this night away,*
*Till the rites of love are ended,*
*And the lusty Bridegroom say,*
*Welcome light of all befriended.*
*Pace out you watry powers below, let your feet*
*Like the Gallies when they row, even beat.*
*Let your unknown measures set*
*To the still winds, tell to all*
*That Gods are come immortal great,*
*To honour this great Nuptial.*

The Measure.   Second Song.

*Hold back thy hours dark night, till we have done,*
*The day will come too soon;*
*Young Maids will curse thee if thou steal'st away,*
*And leav'st their blushes open to the day.*
*Stay, stay, and hide the blushes of the Bride.*
*Stay gentle night, and with thy darkness cover*
*The kisses of her Lover.*
*Stay, and confound her tears, and her shrill cryings,*
*Her weak denials, vows, and often dyings;*
*Stay and hide all, but help not though she call.*

*Nep.*   Great Queen of us and Heaven,
Hear what I bring to make this hour a full one,
If not her measure.

*Cinth.*   Speak Seas King.

*Nep.*   Thy tunes my *Amphitrite* joyes to have,
When they will dance upon the rising wave,
And court me as the sails, my *Trytons* play
Musick to lead a storm, I'le lead the way.

14

Song. Measure.

> To bed, to bed; come *Hymen*, lead the Bride,
>   And lay her by her Husbands side:
>   Bring in the Virgins every one
>   That grieve to lie alone:
> That they may kiss while they may say, a maid,
>   To morrow 'twill be other, kist and said:
>   Hesperus be long a shining,
>   Whilst these Lovers are a twining.

*Eol.*      Ho! *Neptune!*

*Nept.*      *Eolus!*

*Eol.*      The Seas go hie,
         *Boreas* hath rais'd a storm; go and applie
         Thy trident, else I prophesie, ere day
         Many a tall ship will be cast away:
         Descend with all the Gods, and all their power to strike a
         cal[m].

*Cin.*      A thanks to every one, and to gratulate
         So great a service done at my desire,
         Ye shall have many floods fuller and higher
         Than you have wisht for; no Ebb shall dare
         To let the day see where your dwellings are:
         Now back unto your Government in haste,
         Lest your proud charge should swell above the waste,
         And win upon the Island.

*Nep.*      We obey.

                [*Neptune descends, and the Sea-gods.*

*Cinth.*      Hold up thy head dead night; seest thou not day?
         The East begins to lighten, I must down
         And give my brother place.

*Nigh.*      Oh! I could frown
         To see the day, the day that flings his light
         Upon my Kingdoms, and contemns old Night;
         Let him go on and flame, I hope to see

Another wild-fire in his Axletree;
And all false drencht; but I forgot, speak Queen.
The day grows on I must no more be seen.

Cin.    Heave up thy drowsie head agen, and see
          A greater light, a greater Majestie,
          Between our sect and us; whip up thy team;
          The day breaks here, and you some flashing stream
          Shot from the South; say, which way wilt thou go?

Nigh.    I'le vanish into mists.
                              [*Exeunt.*

Cin.    I into day.          [*Finis Mask.*

King.    Take lights there Ladies, get the Bride to bed;
          We will not see you laid, good night *Amintor,*
          We'l ease you of that tedious ceremony;
          Were it [my] case, I should think time run slow.
          If thou beest noble, youth, get me a boy,
          That may defend my Kingdom from my foes.

Amin.    All happiness to you.

King.    Good night *Melantius.*
                              [*Exeunt.*

*Actus Secundus.*

*Enter* Evadne, Aspatia, Dula, *and other Ladies.*

Dul.    Madam, shall we undress you for this fight?
          The Wars are nak'd that you must make to night.

Evad.    You are very merry *Dula.*

Dul.    I should be far merrier Madam, if it were with me as it is with
          you.

Eva.    Why how now wench?

Dul.    Come Ladies will you help?

Eva.    I am soon undone.

Dul.    And as soon done:
          Good store of Cloaths will trouble you at both.

Evad.    Art thou drunk *Dula*?

Dul.    Why here's none but we.

Evad.    Thou think'st belike, there is no modesty
          When we are alone.

Dul.    I by my troth you hit my thoughts aright.

Evad.    You prick me Lady.

Dul.    'Tis against my will,
          Anon you must endure more, and lie still.
          You're best to practise.

Evad.    Sure this wench is mad.

Dul.    No faith, this is a trick that I have had
          Since I was fourteen.

Evad.    'Tis high time to leave it.

*Dul.*       Nay, now I'le keep it till the trick leave me;
           A dozen wanton words put in your head,
           Will make you lively in your Husbands bed.

*Evad.*     Nay faith, then take it.

*Dul.*       Take it Madam, where?
           We all I hope will take it that are here.

*Evad.*     Nay then I'le give you o're.

*Dul.*       So will I make
           The ablest man in *Rhodes*, or his heart to ake.

*Evad.*     Wilt take my place to night?

*Dul.*       I'le hold your Cards against any two I know.

*Evad.*     What wilt thou do?

*Dul.*       Madam, we'l do't, and make'm leave play too.

*Evad.*     *Aspatia*, take her part.

*Dul.*       I will refuse it.
           She will pluck down a side, she does not use it.

*Evad.*     Why, do.

*Dul.*       You will find the play
           Quickly, because your head lies well that way.

*Evad.*     I thank thee *Dula*, would thou could'st instill
           Some of thy mirth into *Aspatia*:
           Nothing but sad thoughts in her breast do dwell,
           Methinks a mean betwixt you would do well.

*Dul.*       She is in love, hang me if I were so,
           But I could run my Country, I love too
           To do those things that people in love do.

*Asp.*      It were a timeless smile should prove my cheek,
           It were a fitter hour for me to laugh,

When at the Altar the Religious Priest
Were pacifying the offended powers
With sacrifice, than now, this should have been
My night, and all your hands have been imployed
In giving me a spotless offering
To young *Amintors* bed, as we are now
For you: pardon *Evadne*, would my worth
Were great as yours, or that the King, or he,
Or both thought so, perhaps he found me worthless,
But till he did so, in these ears of mine,
(These credulous ears) he pour'd the sweetest words
That Art or Love could frame; if he were false,
Pardon it heaven, and if I did want
Vertue, you safely may forgive that too,
For I have left none that I had from you.

*Evad.*     Nay, leave this sad talk Madam.

*Asp.*     Would I could, then should I leave the cause.

*Evad.*     See if you have not spoil'd all *Dulas* mirth.

*Asp.*     Thou think'st thy heart hard, but if thou beest caught, remember me; thou shalt perceive a fire shot suddenly into thee.

*Dul.*     That's not so good, let'm shoot any thing but fire, I fear'm not.

*Asp.*     Well wench, thou mayst be taken.

*Evad.*     Ladies good night, I'le do the rest my self.

*Dul.*     Nay, let your Lord do some.

*Asp.*     Lay a Garland on my Hearse of the dismal Yew.

*Evad.*     That's one of your sad songs Madam.

*Asp.*     Believe me, 'tis a very pretty one.

*Evad.*     How is it Madam?

SONG.

Asp.      *Lay a Garland on my Hearse of the dismal yew;*
           *Maidens, Willow branches bear; say I died true:*
           *My Love was false, but I was firm from my hour of birth;*
           *Upon my buried body lay lightly gentle earth.*

*Evad.*    Fie on't Madam, the words are so strange, they are able to make one Dream of Hobgoblins; *I could never have the power,* Sing that *Dula.*

Dula.    *I could never have the power*
           *To love one above an hour,*
           *But my heart would prompt mine eye*
           *On some other man to flie;*
           Venus, *fix mine eyes fast,*
           *Or if not, give me all that I shall see at last.*

*Evad.*    So, leave me now.

*Dula.*    Nay, we must see you laid.

*Asp.*    Madam good night, may all the marriage joys
           That longing Maids imagine in their beds,
           Prove so unto you; may no discontent
           Grow 'twixt your Love and you; but if there do,
           Enquire of me, and I will guide your moan,
           Teach you an artificial way to grieve,
           To keep your sorrow waking; love your Lord
           No worse than I; but if you love so well,
           Alas, you may displease him, so did I.
           This is the last time you shall look on me:
           Ladies farewel; as soon as I am dead,
           Come all and watch one night about my Hearse;
           Bring each a mournful story and a tear
           To offer at it when I go to earth:
           With flattering Ivie clasp my Coffin round,
           Write on my brow my fortune, let my Bier
           Be born by Virgins that shall sing by course
           The truth of maids and perjuries of men.

*Evad.*    Alas, I pity thee.

                              [*Exit Evadne.*

*Omnes.*  Madam, goodnight.

*1 Lady.*  Come, we'l let in the Bridegroom.

*Dul.*  Where's my Lord?

*1 Lady.*  Here take this light.

[*Enter Amintor.*

*Dul.*  You'l find her in the dark.

*1 Lady.*  Your Lady's scarce a bed yet, you must help her.

*Asp.*  Go and be happy in your Ladies love;
  May all the wrongs that you have done to me,
  Be utterly forgotten in my death.
  I'le trouble you no more, yet I will take
  A parting kiss, and will not be denied.
  You'l come my Lord, and see the Virgins weep
  When I am laid in earth, though you your self
  Can know no pity: thus I wind my self
  Into this willow Garland, and am prouder
  That I was once your Love (though now refus'd)
  Than to have had another true to me.
  So with my prayers I leave you, and must try
  Some yet unpractis'd way to grieve and die.

*Dul.*  Come Ladies, will you go?
             [*Exit Aspatia.*

*Om.*  Goodnight my Lord.

*Amin.*  Much happiness unto you all.

[*Exeunt Ladies.*

  I did that Lady wrong; methinks I feel
  Her grief shoot suddenly through all my veins;
  Mine eyes run; this is strange at such a time.
  It was the King first mov'd me to't, but he
  Has not my will in keeping—why do I
  Perplex my self thus? something whispers me,

21

Go not to bed; my guilt is not so great
As mine own conscience (too sensible)
Would make me think; I only brake a promise,
And 'twas the King that forc't me: timorous flesh,
Why shak'st thou so? away my idle fears.

[*Enter Evadne.*

Yonder she is, the lustre of whose eye
Can blot away the sad remembrance
Of all these things: Oh my *Evadne*, spare
That tender body, let it not take cold,
The vapours of the night will not fall here.
To bed my Love; *Hymen* will punish us
For being slack performers of his rites.
Cam'st thou to call me?

*Evad.*   No.

*Amin.*   Come, come my Love,
          And let us lose our selves to one another.
          Why art thou up so long?

*Evad.*   I am not well.

*Amint.*   To bed then let me wind thee in these arms,
           Till I have banisht sickness.

*Evad.*   Good my Lord, I cannot sleep.

*Amin.*   *Evadne*, we'l watch, I mean no sleeping.

*Evad.*   I'le not go to bed.

*Amin.*   I prethee do.

*Evad.*   I will not for the world.

*Amin.*   Why my dear Love?

*Evad.*   Why? I have sworn I will not.

*Amin.*   Sworn!

The Maids Tragedy

*Evad.*   I.

*Amint.*   How? Sworn *Evadne*?

*Evad.*   Yes, Sworn *Amintor*, and will swear again
     If you will wish to hear me.

*Amin.*   To whom have you Sworn this?

*Evad.*   If I should name him, the matter were not great.

*Amin.*   Come, this is but the coyness of a Bride.

*Evad.*   The coyness of a Bride?

*Amin.*   How prettily that frown becomes thee!

*Evad.*   Do you like it so?

*Amin.*   Thou canst not dress thy face in such a look
     But I shall like it.

*Evad.*   What look likes you best?

*Amin.*   Why do you ask?

*Evad.*   That I may shew you one less pleasing to you.

*Amin.*   How's that?

*Evad.*   That I may shew you one less pleasing to you.

*Amint.*   I prethee put thy jests in milder looks.
     It shews as thou wert angry.

*Evad.*   So perhaps I am indeed.

*Amint.*   Why, who has done thee wrong?
     Name me the man, and by thy self I swear,
     Thy yet unconquer'd self, I will revenge thee.

*Evad.*   Now I shall try thy truth; if thou dost love me,
     Thou weigh'st not any thing compar'd with me;

Life, Honour, joyes Eternal, all Delights
This world can yield, or hopeful people feign,
Or in the life to come, are light as Air
To a true Lover when his Lady frowns,
And bids him do this: wilt thou kill this man?
Swear my *Amintor*, and I'le kiss the sin off from
thy lips.

*Amin.*   I will not swear sweet Love,
        Till I do know the cause.

*Evad.*   I would thou wouldst;
        Why, it is thou that wrongest me, I hate thee,
        Thou shouldst have kill'd thy self.

*Amint.*  If I should know that, I should quickly kill
        The man you hated.

*Evad.*   Know it then, and do't.

*Amint.*  Oh no, what look soe're thou shalt put on,
        To try my faith, I shall not think thee false;
        I cannot find one blemish in thy face,
        Where falsehood should abide: leave and to bed;
        If you have sworn to any of the Virgins
        That were your old companions, to preserve
        Your Maidenhead a night, it may be done without this
        means.

*Evad.*   A Maidenhead *Amintor* at my years?

*Amint.*  Sure she raves, this cannot be
        Thy natural temper; shall I call thy maids?
        Either thy healthful sleep hath left thee long,
        Or else some Fever rages in thy blood.

*Evad.*   Neither *Amintor*; think you I am mad,
        Because I speak the truth?

*Amint.*  Will you not lie with me to night?

*Evad.*   To night? you talk as if I would hereafter.

24

*Amint.*   Hereafter? yes, I do.

*Evad.*   You are deceiv'd, put off amazement, and with patience
mark

What I shall utter, for the Oracle
Knows nothing truer, 'tis not for a night
Or two that I forbear thy bed, but for ever.

*Amint.*   I dream,—awake *Amintor!*

*Evad.*   You hear right,
I sooner will find out the beds of Snakes,
And with my youthful blood warm their cold flesh,
Letting them curle themselves about my Limbs,
Than sleep one night with thee; this is not feign'd,
Nor sounds it like the coyness of a Bride.

*Amin.*   Is flesh so earthly to endure all this?
Are these the joyes of Marriage? *Hymen* keep
This story (that will make succeeding youth
Neglect thy Ceremonies) from all ears.
Let it not rise up for thy shame and mine
To after ages; we will scorn thy Laws,
If thou no better bless them; touch the heart
Of her that thou hast sent me, or the world
Shall know there's not an Altar that will smoak
In praise of thee; we will adopt us Sons;
Then vertue shall inherit, and not blood:
If we do lust, we'l take the next we meet,
Serving our selves as other Creatures do,
And never take note of the Female more,
Nor of her issue. I do rage in vain,
She can but jest; Oh! pardon me my Love;
So dear the thoughts are that I hold of thee,
That I must break forth; satisfie my fear:
It is a pain beyond the hand of death,
To be in doubt; confirm it with an Oath, if this be true.

*Evad.*   Do you invent the form:
Let there be in it all the binding words
Devils and Conjurers can put together,
And I will take it; I have sworn before,
And here by all things holy do again,

Never to be acquainted with thy bed.
Is your doubt over now?

*Amint.*  I know too much, would I had doubted still;
Was ever such a marriage night as this!
You powers above, if you did ever mean
Man should be us'd thus, you have thought a way
How he may bear himself, and save his honour:
Instruct me in it; for to my dull eyes
There is no mean, no moderate course to run,
 I must live scorn'd, or be a murderer:
Is there a third? why is this night so calm?
Why does not Heaven speak in Thunder to us,
And drown her voice?

*Evad.*  This rage will do no good.

*Amint.*  Evadne, hear me, thou hast ta'ne an Oath,
But such a rash one, that to keep it, were
Worse than to swear it; call it back to thee;
Such vows as those never ascend the Heaven;
A tear or two will wash it quite away:
Have mercy on my youth, my hopeful youth,
 If thou be pitiful, for (without boast)
This Land was proud of me: what Lady was there
That men call'd fair and vertuous in this Isle,
That would have shun'd my love? It is in thee
To make me hold this worth—Oh! we vain men
That trust out all our reputation,
To rest upon the weak and yielding hand
Of feeble Women! but thou art not stone;
Thy flesh is soft, and in thine eyes doth dwell
The spirit of Love, thy heart cannot be hard.
Come lead me from the bottom of despair,
To all the joyes thou hast; I know thou wilt;
And make me careful, lest the sudden change
O're-come my spirits.

*Evad.*  When I call back this Oath, the pains of hell inviron me.

*Amin.*  I sleep, and am too temperate; come to bed, or by
Those hairs, which if thou hast a soul like to thy locks,
Were threads for Kings to wear about their arms.

*Evad.*   Why so perhaps they are.

*Amint.*   I'le drag thee to my bed, and make thy tongue
        Undo this wicked Oath, or on thy flesh
        I'le print a thousand wounds to let out life.

*Evad.*   I fear thee not, do what thou dar'st to me;
        Every ill-sounding word, or threatning look
        Thou shew'st to me, will be reveng'd at full.

*Amint.*   It will not sure *Evadne*.

*Evad.*   Do not you hazard that.

*Amint.*   Ha'ye your Champions?

*Evad.*   Alas *Amintor*, thinkst thou I forbear
        To sleep with thee, because I have put on
        A maidens strictness? look upon these cheeks,
        And thou shalt find the hot and rising blood
        Unapt for such a vow; no, in this heart
        There dwels as much desire, and as much will
        To put that wisht act in practice, as ever yet
        Was known to woman, and they have been shown
        Both; but it was the folly of thy youth,
        To think this beauty (to what Land soe're
        It shall be call'd) shall stoop to any second.
        I do enjoy the best, and in that height
        Have sworn to stand or die: you guess the man.

*Amint.*   No, let me know the man that wrongs me so,
        That I may cut his body into motes,
        And scatter it before the Northern wind.

*Evad.*   You dare not strike him.

*Amint.*   Do not wrong me so;
        Yes, if his body were a poysonous plant,
        That it were death to touch, I have a soul
        Will throw me on him.

*Evad.*   Why 'tis the King.

*Amint.*    The King!

*Evad.*    What will you do now?

*Amint.*    'Tis not the King.

*Evad.*    What, did he make this match for dull *Amintor*?

*Amint.*    Oh! thou hast nam'd a word that wipes away
          All thoughts revengeful: in that sacred name,
          The King, there lies a terror: what frail man
          Dares lift his hand against it? let the Gods
          Speak to him when they please;
          Till then let us suffer and wait.

*Evad.*    Why should you fill your self so full of heat,
          And haste so to my bed? I am no Virgin.

*Amint.*    What Devil put it in thy fancy then
          To marry me?

*Evad.*    Alas, I must have one
          To Father Children, and to bear the name
          Of Husband to me, that my sin may be more honourable.

*Amint.*    What a strange thing am I!

*Evad.*    A miserable one; one that my self am sorry for.

*Amint.*    Why shew it then in this,
          If thou hast pity, though thy love be none,
          Kill me, and all true Lovers that shall live
          In after ages crost in their desires,
          Shall bless thy memory, and call thee good,
          Because such mercy in thy heart was found,
          To rid a lingring Wretch.

*Evad.*    I must have one
          To fill thy room again, if thou wert dead,
          Else by this night I would: I pity thee.

*Amint.*    These strange and sudden injuries have faln
          So thick upon me, that I lose all sense

Of what they are: methinks I am not wrong'd,
Nor is it ought, if from the censuring World
I can but hide it—Reputation,
Thou art a word, no more; but thou hast shown
An impudence so high, that to the World
I fear thou wilt betray or shame thy self.

Evad. To cover shame I took thee, never fear
That I would blaze my self.

Amint. Nor let the King
Know I conceive he wrongs me, then mine honour
Will thrust me into action, that my flesh
Could bear with patience; and it is some ease
To me in these extreams, that I knew this
Before I toucht thee; else had all the sins
Of mankind stood betwixt me and the King,
I had gone through 'em to his heart and thine.
I have lost one desire, 'tis not his crown
Shall buy me to thy bed: now I resolve
He has dishonour'd thee; give me thy hand,
Be careful of thy credit, and sin close,
'Tis all I wish; upon thy Chamber-floore
I'le rest to night, that morning visiters
May think we did as married people use.
And prethee smile upon me when they come,
And seem to toy, as if thou hadst been pleas'd
With what we did.

Evad. Fear not, I will do this.

Amint. Come let us practise, and as wantonly
As ever loving Bride and Bridegroom met,
Lets laugh and enter here.

Evad. I am content.

Amint. Down all the swellings of my troubled heart.
When we walk thus intwin'd, let all eyes see
If ever Lovers better did agree.

[*Exit.*

29

*Enter* Aspatia, Antiphila *and* Olympias.

Asp. Away, you are not sad, force it no further;
   Good Gods, how well you look! such a full colour
   Young bashful Brides put on: sure you are new married.

Ant. Yes Madam, to your grief.

Asp. Alas! poor Wenches.
   Go learn to love first, learn to lose your selves,
   Learn to be flattered, and believe, and bless
   The double tongue that did it;
   Make a Faith out of the miracles of Ancient Lovers.
   Did you ne're love yet Wenches? speak *Olympias*,
   Such as speak truth and dy'd in't,
   And like me believe all faithful, and be miserable;
   Thou hast an easie temper, fit for stamp.

Olymp. Never.

Asp. Nor you *Antiphila*?

Ant. Nor I.

Asp. Then my good Girles, be more than Women, wise. At least
   be more than I was; and be sure you credit any thing the
   light gives light to, before a man; rather believe the Sea
   weeps for the ruin'd Merchant when he roars; rather the
   wind courts but the pregnant sails when the strong
   cordage cracks; rather the Sun comes but to kiss the Fruit
   in wealthy Autumn, when all falls blasted; if you needs
   must love (forc'd by ill fate) take to your maiden bosoms
   two dead cold aspicks, and of them make Lovers, they
   cannot flatter nor forswear; one kiss makes a long peace
   for all; but man, Oh that beast man!
   Come lets be sad my Girles;
   That down cast of thine eye, *Olympias*,
   Shews a fine sorrow; mark *Antiphila*,
   Just such another was the Nymph *Oenone*,
   When *Paris* brought home *Helen*: now a tear,
   And then thou art a piece expressing fully
   The *Carthage* Queen, when from a cold Sea Rock,
   Full with her sorrow, she tyed fast her eyes

To the fair *Trojan* ships, and having lost them,
Just as thine eyes do, down stole a tear, *Antiphila*;
What would this Wench do, if she were *Aspatia*?
Here she would stand, till some more pitying God
Turn'd her to Marble: 'tis enough my Wench;
Shew me the piece of Needle-work you wrought.

*Ant.*    Of *Ariadne*, Madam?

*Asp.*    Yes that piece.
This should be *Theseus*, h'as a cousening face,
You meant him for a man.

*Ant.*    He was so Madam.

*Asp.*    Why then 'tis well enough, never look back,
You have a full wind, and a false heart *Theseus*;
Does not the story say, his Keel was split,
Or his Masts spent, or some kind rock or other
Met with his Vessel?

*Ant.*    Not as I remember.

*Asp.*    It should ha' been so; could the Gods know this,
And not of all their number raise a storm?
But they are all as ill. This false smile was well exprest;
Just such another caught me; you shall not go
so *Antiphila*,
In this place work a quick-sand,
And over it a shallow smiling Water.
And his ship ploughing it, and then a fear.
Do that fear to the life Wench.

*Ant.*    'Twill wrong the story.

*Asp.*    'Twill make the story wrong'd by wanton Poets
Live long and be believ'd; but where's the Lady?

*Ant.*    There Madam.

*Asp.*    Fie, you have mist it here *Antiphila*,
You are much mistaken Wench;
These colours are not dull and pale enough,

To shew a soul so full of misery
As this sad Ladies was; do it by me,
Do it again by me the lost *Aspatia*,
And you shall find all true but the wild Island;
I stand upon the Sea breach now, and think
Mine arms thus, and mine hair blown with the wind,
Wild as that desart, and let all about me
Tell that I am forsaken, do my face

(If thou hadst ever feeling of a sorrow)
Thus, thus, *Antiphila* strive to make me look
Like sorrows monument; and the trees about me,
Let them be dry and leaveless; let the Rocks
Groan with continual surges, and behind me
Make all a desolation; look, look Wenches,
A miserable life of this poor Picture.

*Olym.*　Dear Madam!

*Asp.*　I have done, sit down, and let us
　　　Upon that point fix all our eyes, that point there;
　　　Make a dull silence till you feel a sudden sadness
　　　Give us new souls.
　　　　　　　　　　[*Enter Calianax.*

*Cal.*　The King may do this, and he may not do it;
　　　My child is wrong'd, disgrac'd: well, how now Huswives?
　　　What at your ease? is this a time to sit still? up you young
　　　Lazie Whores, up or I'le sweng you.

*Olym.*　Nay, good my Lord.

*Cal.*　You'l lie down shortly, get you in and work;
　　　What are you grown so resty? you want ears,
　　　We shall have some of the Court boys do that Office.

*Ant.*　My Lord we do no more than we are charg'd:
　　　It is the Ladies pleasure we be thus in grief;
　　　She is forsaken.

　　　*Cal.* There's a Rogue too,
　　　A young dissembling slave; well, get you in,
　　　I'le have a bout with that boy; 'tis high time

Now to be valiant; I confess my youth
Was never prone that way: what, made an Ass?
A Court stale? well I will be valiant,
And beat some dozen of these Whelps; I will; and there's
Another of 'em, a trim cheating souldier,
I'le maul that Rascal, h'as out-brav'd me twice;
But now I thank the Gods I am valiant;
Go, get you in, I'le take a course with all.

[*Exeunt Omnes.*

*Actus Tertius.*

*Enter* Cleon, Strato, Diphilus.

*Cle.*    Your sister is not up yet.

*Diph.*   Oh, Brides must take their mornings rest,
          The night is troublesome.

*Stra.*   But not tedious.

*Diph.*   What odds, he has not my Sisters maiden-head to night?

*Stra.*   No, it's odds against any Bridegroom living, he ne're gets it
          while he lives.

*Diph.*   Y'are merry with my Sister, you'l please to allow me the
          same freedom with your Mother.

*Stra.*   She's at your service.

*Diph.*   Then she's merry enough of her self, she needs no tickling;
          knock at the door.

*Stra.*   We shall interrupt them.

*Diph.*   No matter, they have the year before them.
          Good morrow Sister; spare your self to day, the night will
          come again.

                    [*Enter Amintor.*

*Amint.*  Who's there, my Brother? I am no readier yet, your Sister is
          but now up.

*Diph.*   You look as you had lost your eyes to night; I think you ha'
          not slept.

*Amint.*  I faith I have not.

*Diph.*   You have done better then.

*Amint.* We ventured for a Boy; when he is Twelve,
　　　He shall command against the foes of *Rhodes*.

*Stra.* You cannot, you want sleep.
　　　　　　　　　　　[*Aside.*

*Amint.* 'Tis true; but she
　　　As if she had drunk *Lethe*, or had made
　　　Even with Heaven, did fetch so still a sleep,
　　　So sweet and sound.

*Diph.* What's that?

*Amint.* Your Sister frets this morning, and does turn her eyes upon
　　　me, as people on their headsman; she does chafe, and kiss,
　　　and chafe again, and clap my cheeks; she's in another
　　　world.

*Diph.* Then I had lost; I was about to lay, you had not got her
　　　Maiden-head to night.

*Amint.* Ha! he does not mock me; y'ad lost indeed;
　　　I do not use to bungle.

*Cleo.* You do deserve her.

*Amint.* I laid my lips to hers, and [t]hat wild breath
　　　That was rude and rough to me, last night

　　　　　　　　　　　[*Aside.*

　　　Was sweet as *April*; I'le be guilty too,
　　　If these be the effects.

　　　　　　　　[*Enter Melantius.*

*Mel.* Good day *Amintor*, for to me the name
　　　Of Brother is too distant; we are friends,
　　　And that is nearer.

*Amint.* Dear *Melantius*!
　　　Let me behold thee; is it possible?

35

*Mel.*     What sudden gaze is this?

*Amint.*  'Tis wonderous strange.

*Mel.*     Why does thine eye desire so strict a view
           Of that it knows so well?
           There's nothing here that is not thine.

*Amint.*  I wonder much *Melantius*,
           To see those noble looks that make me think
           How vertuous thou art; and on the sudden
           'Tis strange to me, thou shouldst have worth and honour,
           Or not be base, and false, and treacherous,
           And every ill. But—

*Mel.*     Stay, stay my Friend,
           I fear this sound will not become our loves; no more,
           embrace me.

*Amint.*  Oh mistake me not;
           I know thee to be full of all those deeds
           That we frail men call good: but by the course
           Of nature thou shouldst be as quickly chang'd
           As are the winds, dissembling as the Sea,
           That now wears brows as smooth as Virgins be,
           Tempting the Merchant to invade his face,
           And in an hour calls his billows up,
           And shoots 'em at the Sun, destroying all
           He carries on him. O how near am I

                        [*Aside.*

           To utter my sick thoughts!

*Mel.*     But why, my Friend, should I be so by Nature?

*Amin.*  I have wed thy Sister, who hath vertuous thoughts
           Enough for one whole family, and it is strange
           That you should feel no want.

*Mel.*     Believe me, this complement's too cunning for me.

*Diph.*  What should I be then by the course of nature,

They having both robb'd me of so much vertue?

*Strat.*     O call the Bride, my Lord *Amintor*, that we may see her blush, and turn her eyes down; it is the prettiest sport.

*Amin.*     *Evadne*!

*Evad.*     My Lord!
                                    [*Within.*

*Amint.*   Come forth my Love,
           Your Brothers do attend to wish you joy.

*Evad.*     I am not ready yet.

*Amint.*   Enough, enough.

*Evad.*     They'l mock me.

*Amint.*   Faith thou shalt come in.

                      [*Enter Evadne.*

*Mel.*     Good morrow Sister; he that understands
           Whom you have wed, need not to wish you joy.
           You have enough, take heed you be not proud.

*Diph.*     O Sister, what have you done!

*Evad.*     I done! why, what have I done?

*Strat.*     My Lord *Amintor* swears you are no Maid now.

*Evad.*     Push!

*Strat.*     I faith he does.

*Evad.*     I knew I should be mockt.

*Diph.*     With a truth.

*Evad.*     If 'twere to do again, in faith I would not marry.

*Amint.*  Not I by Heaven.

[Aside.

*Diph.*  Sister, Dula swears she heard you cry two rooms off.

*Evad.*  Fie how you talk!

*Diph.*  Let's see you walk.

*Evad.*  By my troth y'are spoil'd.

*Mel.*  *Amintor*!

*Amint.*  Ha!

*Mel.*  Thou art sad.

*Amint.*  Who I? I thank you for that, shall *Diphilus*, thou and I sing a catch?

*Mel.*  How!

*Amint.*  Prethee let's.

*Mel.*  Nay, that's too much the other way.

*Amint.*  I am so lightned with my happiness: how dost thou Love? kiss me.

*Evad.*  I cannot love you, you tell tales of me.

*Amint.*  Nothing but what becomes us: Gentlemen,
Would you had all such Wives, and all the world,
That I might be no wonder; y'are all sad;
What, do you envie me? I walk methinks
On water, and ne're sink, I am so light.

*Mel.*  'Tis well you are so.

*Amint.*  Well? how can I be other, when she looks thus?
Is there no musick there? let's dance.

*Mel.*  Why? this is strange, *Amintor*!

*Amint.*  I do not know my self;
        Yet I could wish my joy were less.

*Diph.*  I'le marry too, if it will make one thus.

*Evad.*  *Amintor*, hark.                    [*Aside.*

*Amint.*  What says my Love? I must obey.

*Evad.*  You do it scurvily, 'twill be perceiv'd.

*Cle.*  My Lord the King is here.

                    [*Enter King and Lysi.*

*Amint.*  Where?

*Stra.*  And his Brother.

*King.*  Good morrow all.
        *Amintor*, joy on, joy fall thick upon thee!
        And Madam, you are alter'd since I saw you,
        I must salute you; you are now anothers;
        How lik't you your nights rest?

*Evad.*  Ill Sir.

*Amint.*  I! 'deed she took but little.

*Lys.*  You'l let her take more, and thank her too shortly.

*King.*  *Amintor*, wert thou truly honest
        Till thou wert Married?

*Amint.*  Yes Sir.

*King.*  Tell me then, how shews the sport unto thee?

*Amint.*  Why well.

*King.*  What did you do?

*Amint.*  No more nor less than other couples use;

You know what 'tis; it has but a course name.

*King.* But prethee, I should think by her black eye,
And her red cheek, she should be quick and stirring
In this same business, ha?

*Amint.* I cannot tell, I ne're try'd other Sir, but I perceive
She is as quick as you delivered.

*King.* Well, you'l trust me then *Amintor*,
To choose a Wife for you agen?

*Amint.* No never Sir.

*King.* Why? like you this so ill?

*Amint.* So well I like her.
For this I bow my knee in thanks to you,
And unto Heaven will pay my grateful tribute
Hourly, and to hope we shall draw out
A long contented life together here,
And die both full of gray hairs in one day;
For which the thanks is yours; but if the powers
That rule us, please to call her first away,
Without pride spoke, this World holds not a Wife
Worthy to take her room.

*King.* I do not like this; all forbear the room
But you *Amintor* and your Lady. I have some speech with
You, that may concern your after living well.
*Amint.* He will not tell me that he lies with her: if
he do, Something Heavenly stay my heart, for I shall be apt
To thrust this arm of mine to acts unlawful.

*King.* You will suffer me to talk with her *Amintor*,
And not have a jealous pang!

*Amint.* Sir, I dare trust my Wife
With whom she dares to talk, and not be jealous.

*King.* How do you like *Amintor*?

*Evad.* As I did Sir.

*King.*   How's that!

*Evad.*   As one that to fulfil your will and pleasure,
      I have given leave to call me Wife and Love.

*King.*   I see there is no lasting Faith in Sin;
      They that break word with Heaven, will break again
      With all the World, and so dost thou with me.

*Evad.*   How Sir?

*King.*   This subtile Womans ignorance
      Will not excuse you; thou hast taken Oaths
      So great, methought they did not well become
      A Womans mouth, that thou wouldst ne're enjoy
      A man but me.

*Evad.*   I never did swear so; you do me wrong.

*King.*   Day and night have heard it.

*Evad.*   I swore indeed that I would never love
      A man of lower place; but if your fortune
      Should throw you from this height, I bade you trust
      I would forsake you, and would bend to him
      That won your Throne; I love with my ambition,
      Not with mine eyes; but if I ever yet
      Toucht any other, Leprosie light here
      Upon my face, which for your Royalty I would not stain.

*King.*   Why thou dissemblest, and it is in me to punish thee.

*Evad.*   Why, it is in me then not to love you, which will
      More afflict your body, than your punishment can mine.

*King.*   But thou hast let *Amintor* lie with thee.

*Evad.*   I ha'not.

*King.*   Impudence! he saies himself so.

*Evad.*   He lyes.

*King.*   He does not.

*Evad.*   By this light he does, strangely and basely, and
        I'le prove it so; I did not shun him for a night,
        But told him I would never close with him.

 *King.*   Speak lower, 'tis false.

*Evad.*    I'm no man to answer with a blow;
        Or if I were, you are the King; but urge me not, 'tis most
        true.

*King.*   Do not I know the uncontrouled thoughts
        That youth brings with him, when his bloud is high
        With expectation and desires of that
        He long hath waited for? is not his spirit,
        Though he be temperate, of a valiant strain,
        As this our age hath known? what could he do,
        If such a sudden speech had met his blood,
        But ruine thee for ever? if he had not kill'd thee,
        He could not bear it thus; he is as we,
        Or any other wrong'd man.

*Evad.*   It is dissembling.

*King.*   Take him; farewel; henceforth I am thy foe;
        And what disgraces I can blot thee, look for.

*Evad.*   Stay Sir; *Amintor*, you shall hear, *Amintor*.

*Amint.*   What my Love?

*Evad.*   *Amintor*, thou hast an ingenious look,
        And shouldst be vertuous; it amazeth me,
        That thou canst make such base malicious lyes.

*Amint.*   What my dear Wife?

*Evad.*   Dear Wife! I do despise thee;
        Why, nothing can be baser, than to sow
        Dissention amongst Lovers.

*Amint.*   Lovers! who?

*Evad.*    The King and me.

*Amint.*  O Heaven!

*Evad.*      Who should live long, and love without distaste,
            Were it not for such pickthanks as thy self!
            Did you lie with me? swear now, and be punisht in hell
            For this.

*Amint.*  The faithless Sin I made
            To fair *Aspatia*, is not yet reveng'd,
            It follows me; I will not lose a word
            To this wild Woman; but to you my King,
            The anguish of my soul thrusts out this truth,
            Y'are a Tyrant; and not so much to wrong
            An honest man thus, as to take a pride
            In talking with him of it.

*Evad.*     Now Sir, see how loud this fellow lyed.

*Amint.*  You that can know to wrong, should know how
            Men must right themselves: what punishment is due
            From me to him that shall abuse my bed!
            It is not death; nor can that satisfie,
            Unless I send your lives through all the Land,
            To shew how nobly I have freed my self.

*King.*     Draw not thy Sword, thou knowest I cannot fear
            A subjects hand; but thou shalt feel the weight of this
            If thou dost rage.

*Amint.*  The weight of that?
            If you have any worth, for Heavens sake think
            I fear not Swords; for as you are meer man,
            I dare as easily kill you for this deed,
            As you dare think to do it; but there is
            Divinity about you, that strikes dead
            My rising passions, as you are my King,
            I fall before you, and present my Sword
            To cut mine own flesh, if it be your will.
            Alas! I am nothing but a multitude
            Of walking griefs; yet should I murther you,
            I might before the world take the excuse

Of madness: for compare my injuries,
And they will well appear too sad a weight
For reason to endure; but fall I first
Amongst my sorrows, ere my treacherous hand
Touch holy things: but why? I know not what
I have to say; why did you choose out me
To make thus wretched? there were thousand fools
Easie to work on, and of state enough within the Island.

*Evad.*   I would not have a fool, it were no credit for me.

*Amint.*  Worse and worse!
Thou that dar'st talk unto thy Husband thus,
Profess thy self a Whore; and more than so,
Resolve to be so still; it is my fate
To bear and bow beneath a thousand griefs,
To keep that little credit with the World.
But there were wise ones too, you might have ta'ne
another.

*King.*   No; for I believe thee honest, as thou wert valiant.

*Amint.*  All the happiness
Bestow'd upon me, turns into disgrace;
Gods take your honesty again, for I
Am loaden with it; good my Lord the King, be private
in it.

*King.*   Thou may'st live *Amintor*,
Free as thy King, if thou wilt wink at this,
And be a means that we may meet in secret.

*Amint.*  A Baud! hold my breast, a bitter curse
Seize me, if I forget not all respects
That are Religious, on another word
Sounded like that, and through a Sea of sins
Will wade to my revenge, though I should call
Pains here, and after life upon my soul.

*King.*   Well I am resolute you lay not with her,
And so leave you.

[*Exit King.*

The Maids Tragedy

*Evad.*    You must be prating, and see what follows.

*Amint.*   Prethee vex me not.
          Leave me, I am afraid some sudden start
          Will pull a murther on me.

*Evad.*    I am gone; I love my life well.

                    *[Exit Evadne.*

*Amint.*   I hate mine as much.
          This 'tis to break a troth; I should be glad
          If all this tide of grief would make me mad.

                    *[Exit.*

Enter Melantius.

*Mel.*     I'le know the cause of all *Amintors* griefs,
          Or friendship shall be idle.

               *[Enter Calianax.*

*Cal.*     O *Melantius*, my Daughter will die.

*Mel.*     Trust me, I am sorry; would thou hadst ta'ne her room.

*Cal.*      Thou art a slave, a cut-throat slave, a bloody treacherous
          slave.

*Melan.*  Take heed old man, thou wilt be heard to rave,
          And lose thine Offices.

*Cal.*     I am valiant grown
          At all these years, and thou art but a slave.

*Mel.*     Leave, some company will come, and I respect
          Thy years, not thee so much, that I could wish
          To laugh at thee alone.

*Cal.*     I'le spoil your mirth, I mean to fight with thee;
          There lie my Cloak, this was my Fathers Sword,
          And he durst fight; are you prepar'd?

*Mel.*  Why? wilt thou doat thy self out of thy life?
        Hence get thee to bed, have careful looking to, and eat
        warm things, and trouble not me: my head is full of
        thoughts more weighty than thy life or death can be.

*Cal.*  You have a name in War, when you stand safe
        Amongst a multitude; but I will try
        What you dare do unto a weak old man
        In single fight; you'l ground I fear: Come draw.

*Mel.*  I will not draw, unless thou pul'st thy death
        Upon thee with a stroke; there's no one blow
        That thou canst give, hath strength enough to kill me.
        Tempt me not so far then; the power of earth
        Shall not redeem thee.

*Cal.*  I must let him alone,
        He's stout and able; and to say the truth,
        However I may set a face, and talk,
        I am not valiant: when I was a youth,
        I kept my credit with a testie trick I had,
        Amongst cowards, but durst never fight.

*Mel.*  I will not promise to preserve your life if you do stay.

*Cal.*  I would give half my Land that I durst fight with that proud
        man a little: if I had men to hold, I would beat him, till he
        ask me mercy.

*Mel.*  Sir, will you be gone?

*Cal.*  I dare not stay, but I will go home, and beat my servants all
        over for this.

                        [*Exit Calianax.*

*Mel.*  This old fellow haunts me,
        But the distracted carriage of mine *Amintor*
        Takes deeply on me, I will find the cause;
        I fear his Conscience cries, he wrong'd *Aspatia*.

*Enter Amintor.*

46

*Amint.* Mens eyes are not so subtil to perceive
      My inward misery; I bear my grief
      Hid from the World; how art thou wretched then?
      For ought I know, all Husbands are like me;
      And every one I talk with of his Wife,
      Is but a well dissembler of his woes
      As I am; would I knew it, for the rareness afflicts me now.

*Mel.*     *Amintor,* We have not enjoy'd our friendship of late, for we
      were wont to charge our souls in talk.

*Amint.* *Melantius,* I can tell thee a good jest of *Strato* and a Lady the
      last day.

*Mel.*     How wast?

*Amint.* Why such an odd one.

*Mel.*     I have long'd to speak with you, not of an idle jest that's
      forc'd, but of matter you are bound to utter to me.

*Amint.* What is that my friend?

*Mel.*     I have observ'd, your words fall from your tongue
      Wildly; and all your carriage,
      Like one that strove to shew his merry mood,
      When he were ill dispos'd: you were not wont
      To put such scorn into your speech, or wear
      Upon your face ridiculous jollity:
      Some sadness sits here, which your cunning would
      Cover o're with smiles, and 'twill not be. What is it?

*Amint.* A sadness here! what cause
      Can fate provide for me, to make me so?
      Am I not lov'd through all this Isle? the King
      Rains greatness on me: have I not received
      A Lady to my bed, that in her eye
      Keeps mounting fire, and on her tender cheeks
      Inevitable colour, in her heart
      A prison for all vertue? are not you,
      Which is above all joyes, my constant friend?
      What sadness can I have? no, I am light,
      And feel the courses of my blood more warm

        And stirring than they were; faith marry too,
        And you will feel so unexprest a joy
        In chast embraces, that you will indeed appear another.

*Mel.*    You may shape, *Amintor*,
        Causes to cozen the whole world withal,
        And your self too; but 'tis not like a friend,
        To hide your soul from me; 'tis not your nature
        To be thus idle; I have seen you stand
        As you were blasted; midst of all your mirth,
        Call thrice aloud, and then start, feigning joy
        So coldly: World! what do I here? a friend
        Is nothing, Heaven! I would ha' told that man
        My secret sins; I'le search an unknown Land,
        And there plant friendship, all is withered here;
        Come with a complement, I would have fought,
        Or told my friend he ly'd, ere sooth'd him so;
        Out of my bosom.

*Amint.*  But there is nothing.

*Mel.*    Worse and worse; farewel;
        From this time have acquaintance, but no friend.

*Amint.*  *Melantius*, stay, you shall know what that is.

*Mel.*    See how you play'd with friendship; be advis'd
        How you give cause unto your self to say, You ha'lost a
        friend.

*Amint.*  Forgive what I have done;
        For I am so ore-gone with injuries
        Unheard of, that I lose consideration
        Of what I ought to do—oh—oh.

*Mel.*    Do not weep; what is't?
        May I once but know the man
        Hath turn'd my friend thus?

*Amint.*  I had spoke at first, but that.

*Mel.*    But what?

*Amint.* I held it most unfit
      For you to know; faith do not know it yet.

*Mel.* Thou seest my love, that will keep company
      With thee in tears; hide nothing then from me;
      For when I know the cause of thy distemper,
      With mine own armour I'le adorn my self,
      My resolution, and cut through thy foes,
      Unto thy quiet, till I place thy heart
      As peaceable as spotless innocence. What is it?

*Amint.* Why, 'tis this—it is too big
      To get out, let my tears make way a while.

*Mel.* Punish me strangely heaven, if he escape
      Of life or fame, that brought this youth to this.

*Amint.* Your Sister.

*Mel.* Well said.

*Amint.* You'l wish't unknown, when you have heard it.

*Mel.* No.

*Amint.* Is much to blame,
      And to the King has given her honour up,
      And lives in Whoredom with him.

*Mel.* How, this!
      Thou art run mad with injury indeed,
      Thou couldst not utter this else; speak again,
      For I forgive it freely; tell thy griefs.

*Amint.* She's wanton; I am loth to say a Whore,
      Though it be true.

*Mel.* Speak yet again, before mine anger grow
      Up beyond throwing down; what are thy griefs?

*Amint.* By all our friendship, these.

*Mel.* What? am I tame?

The Maids Tragedy

> After mine actions, shall the name of friend
> Blot all our family, and strike the brand
> Of Whore upon my Sister unreveng'd?
> My shaking flesh be thou a Witness for me,
> With what unwillingness I go to scourge
> This Rayler, whom my folly hath call'd Friend;
> I will not take thee basely; thy sword
> Hangs near thy hand, draw it, that I may whip
> Thy rashness to repentance; draw thy sword.

*Amint.* Not on thee, did thine anger swell as high
As the wild surges; thou shouldst do me ease
Here, and Eternally, if thy noble hand
Would cut me from my sorrows.

*Mel.* This is base and fearful! they that use to utter lyes,
Provide not blows, but words to qualifie
The men they wrong'd; thou hast a guilty cause.

*Amint.* Thou pleasest me; for so much more like this,
Will raise my anger up above my griefs,
Which is a passion easier to be born,
And I shall then be happy.

*Mel.* Take then more to raise thine anger. 'Tis meer
Cowardize makes thee not draw; and I will leave thee
dead
However; but if thou art so much prest
With guilt and fear, as not to dare to fight,
I'le make thy memory loath'd, and fix a scandal
Upon thy name for ever.

*Amint.* Then I draw,
As justly as our Magistrates their Swords,
To cut offenders off; I knew before
'Twould grate your ears; but it was base in you
To urge a weighty secret from your friend,
And then rage at it; I shall be at ease
If I be kill'd; and if you fall by me,
I shall not long out-live you.

*Mel.* Stay a while.
The name of friend is more than family,

Or all the world besides; I was a fool.
Thou searching humane nature, that didst wake
To do me wrong, thou art inquisitive,
And thrusts me upon questions that will take
My sleep away; would I had died ere known
This sad dishonour; pardon me my friend;
If thou wilt strike, here is a faithful heart,
Pierce it, for I will never heave my hand
To thine; behold the power thou hast in me!
I do believe my Sister is a Whore,
A Leprous one, put up thy sword young man.

*Amint.* How should I bear it then, she being so?
I fear my friend that you will lose me shortly;
And I shall do a foul action my self
Through these disgraces.

*Mel.* Better half the Land
Were buried quick together; no, *Amintor,*
Thou shalt have ease: O this Adulterous King
That drew her to't! where got he the spirit
To wrong me so?

*Amint.* What is it then to me,
If it be wrong to you!

*Mel.* Why, not so much: the credit of our house
Is thrown away;
But from his Iron Den I'le waken death,
And hurle him on this King; my honesty
Shall steel my sword, and on its horrid point
I'le wear my cause, that shall amaze the eyes
Of this proud man, and be too glittering
For him to look on.

*Amint.* I have quite undone my fame.

*Mel.* Dry up thy watry eyes,
And cast a manly look upon my face;
For nothing is so wild as I thy friend
Till I have freed thee; still this swelling breast;
I go thus from thee, and will never cease
My vengeance, till I find my heart at peace.

51

*Amint.*  It must not be so; stay, mine eyes would tell
How loth I am to this; but love and tears
Leave me a while, for I have hazarded
All this world calls happy; thou hast wrought
A secret from me under name of Friend,
Which Art could ne're have found, nor torture wrung
From out my bosom; give it me agen,
For I will find it, wheresoe're it lies
Hid in the mortal'st part; invent a way to give it back.

*Mel.*  Why, would you have it back?
I will to death pursue him with revenge.

*Amint.*  Therefore I call it back from thee; for I know
Thy blood so high, that thou wilt stir in this, and shame me
To posterity: take to thy Weapon.

*Mel.*  Hear thy friend, that bears more years than thou.

*Amint.*  I will not hear: but draw, or I— —

*Mel.*  *Amintor.*

*Amint.*  Draw then, for I am full as resolute
As fame and honour can inforce me be;
I cannot linger, draw.

*Mel.*  I do—but is not
My share of credit equal with thine if I do stir?

*Amint.*  No; for it will be cal'd
Honour in thee to spill thy Sisters blood,
If she her birth abuse, and on the King
A brave revenge: but on me that have walkt
With patience in it, it will fix the name
Of fearful Cuckold—O that word! be quick.

*Mel.*  Then joyn with me.

*Amint.*  I dare not do a sin, or else I would: be speedy.

*Mel.*  Then dare not fight with me, for that's a sin.
His grief distracts him; call thy thoughts agen,

And to thy self pronounce the name of friend,
And see what that will work; I will not fight.

*Amint.* You must.

*Mel.* I will be kill'd first, though my passions
Offred the like to you; 'tis not this earth
Shall buy my reason to it; think a while,
For you are (I must weep when I speak that)
Almost besides your self.

*Amint.* Oh my soft temper!
So many sweet words from thy Sisters mouth,
I am afraid would make me take her
To embrace, and pardon her. I am mad indeed,
And know not what I do; yet have a care
Of me in what thou doest.

*Mel.* Why thinks my friend I will forget his honour, or to save
The bravery of our house, will lose his fame,
And fear to touch the Throne of Majesty?

*Amint.* A curse will follow that, but rather live
And suffer with me.

*Mel.* I will do what worth shall bid me, and no more.

*Amint.* Faith I am sick, and desperately I hope,
Yet leaning thus, I feel a kind of ease.

*Mel.* Come take agen your mirth about you.

*Amint.* I shall never do't.

*Mel.* I warrant you, look up, wee'l walk together,
Put thine arm here, all shall be well agen.

*Amint.* Thy Love, O wretched, I thy Love, *Melantius*;
why, I have nothing else.

*Mel.* Be merry then.

[*Exeunt. Enter Melantius agen.*

53

*Mel.*    This worthy young man may do violence
      Upon himself, but I have cherisht him
      To my best power, and sent him smiling from me
      To counterfeit again; Sword hold thine edge,
      My heart will never fail me: *Diphilus*,
      Thou com'st as sent.

                   [*Enter Diphilus.*

*Diph.*   Yonder has been such laughing.

*Mel.*    Betwixt whom?

*Diph.*   Why, our Sister and the King,
      I thought their spleens would break,
      They laught us all out of the room.

*Mel.*    They must weep, *Diphilus*.

*Diph.*   Must they?

*Mel.*    They must: thou art my Brother, and if I did believe
      Thou hadst a base thought, I would rip it out,
      Lie where it durst.

*Diph.*   You should not, I would first mangle my self and find it.

*Mel.*    That was spoke according to our strain; come
      Joyn thy hands to mine,
      And swear a firmness to what project I shall lay before
      thee.

*Diph.*   You do wrong us both;
      People hereafter shall not say there past
      A bond more than our loves, to tie our lives
      And deaths together.

*Mel.*    It is as nobly said as I would wish;
      Anon I'le tell you wonders; we are wrong'd.

*Diph.*   But I will tell you now, wee'l right our selves.

*Mel.*    Stay not, prepare the armour in my house;

And what friends you can draw unto our side,
Not knowing of the cause, make ready too;
Haste *Diphilus*, the time requires it, haste.

[*Exit Diphilus.*

I hope my cause is just, I know my blood
Tells me it is, and I will credit it:
To take revenge, and lose my self withal,
Were idle; and to scape impossible,
Without I had the fort, which misery
Remaining in the hands of my old enemy
*Calianax*, but I must have it, see

[*Enter Calianax.*

Where he comes shaking by me: good my Lord,
Forget your spleen to me, I never wrong'd you,
But would have peace with every man.

Cal.    'Tis well;
        If I durst fight, your tongue would lie at quiet.

Mel.    Y'are touchie without all cause.

Cal.    Do, mock me.

Mel.    By mine honour I speak truth.

Cal.    Honour? where is't?

Mel.    See what starts you make into your hatred to my
        love and freedom to you. —
        I come with resolution to obtain a suit of you.

Cal.    A suit of me! 'tis very like it should be granted, Sir.

Mel.    Nay, go not hence;
        'Tis this; you have the keeping of the Fort,
        And I would wish you by the love you ought
        To bear unto me, to deliver it into my hands.

Cal.    I am in hope that thou art mad, to talk to me thus.

*Mel.*   But there is a reason to move you to it. I would kill the King
        that wrong'd you and your daughter.

*Cal.*   Out Traytor!

*Mel.*   Nay but stay; I cannot scape, the deed once done,
        Without I have this fort.

*Cal.*   And should I help thee? now thy treacherous mind betrays it
        self.

*Mel.*   Come, delay me not;
        Give me a sudden answer, or already
        Thy last is spoke; refuse not offered love,
        When it comes clad in secrets.

*Cal.*   If I say I will not, he will kill me, I do see't writ
        In his looks; and should I say I will, he'l run and tell the
        King: I do not shun your friendship dear *Melantius,*
        But this cause is weighty, give me but an hour to think.

*Mel.*   Take it—I know this goes unto the King,
        But I am arm'd.
                                [*Ex. Melant.*

*Cal.*   Me thinks I feel my self
        But twenty now agen; this fighting fool
        Wants Policy; I shall revenge my Girl,
        And make her red again; I pray, my legs
        Will last that pace that I will carry them,
        I shall want breath before I find the King.

## Actus Quartus.

*Enter* Melantius, Evadne, *and a* Lady.

*Mel.*    Save you.

*Evad.*    Save you sweet Brother.

*Mel.*    In my blunt eye methinks you look *Evadne*.

*Evad.*    Come, you would make me blush.

*Mel.*    I would *Evadne*, I shall displease my ends else.

*Evad.*    You shall if you command me; I am bashful;
         Come Sir, how do I look?

*Mel.*    I would not have your women hear me
         Break into commendation of you, 'tis not seemly.

*Evad.*    Go wait me in the Gallery — now speak.

*Mel.*    I'le lock the door first.

                    [*Exeunt Ladies.*

*Evad.*    Why?

*Mel.*    I will not have your guilded things that dance in
         visitation with their Millan skins choke up my business.

*Evad.*    You are strangely dispos'd Sir.

*Mel.*    Good Madam, not to make you merry.

*Evad.*    No, if you praise me, 'twill make me sad.

*Mel.*    Such a sad commendation I have for you.

*Evad.*    Brother, the Court hath made you witty,
         And learn to riddle.

| | |
|---|---|
| *Mel.* | I praise the Court for't; has it learned you nothing? |
| *Evad.* | Me? |
| *Mel.* | I *Evadne*, thou art young and handsom,<br>A Lady of a sweet complexion,<br>And such a flowing carriage, that it cannot<br>Chuse but inflame a Kingdom. |
| *Evad.* | Gentle Brother! |
| *Mel.* | 'Tis yet in thy remembrance, foolish woman,<br>To make me gentle. |
| *Evad.* | How is this? |
| *Mel.* | 'Tis base,<br>And I could blush at these years, through all<br>My honour'd scars, to come to such a parly. |
| *Evad.* | I understand you not. |
| *Mel.* | You dare not, Fool;<br>They that commit thy faults, fly the remembrance. |
| *Evad.* | My faults, Sir! I would have you know I care not<br>If they were written here, here in my forehead. |
| *Mel.* | Thy body is too little for the story,<br>The lusts of which would fill another woman,<br>Though she had Twins within her. |
| *Evad.* | This is saucy;<br>Look you intrude no more, there lies your way. |
| *Mel.* | Thou art my way, and I will tread upon thee,<br>Till I find truth out. |
| *Evad.* | What truth is that you look for? |
| *Mel.* | Thy long-lost honour: would the Gods had set me<br>One of their loudest bolts; come tell me quickly,<br>Do it without enforcement, and take heed |

# The Maids Tragedy

You swell me not above my temper.

*Evad.*　How Sir? where got you this report?

*Mel.*　Where there was people in every place.

*Evad.*　They and the seconds of it are base people;
　　　　Believe them not, they lyed.

*Mel.*　Do not play with mine anger, do not Wretch,
　　　　I come to know that desperate Fool that drew thee
　　　　From thy fair life; be wise, and lay him open.

*Evad.*　Unhand me, and learn manners, such another
　　　　Forgetfulness forfeits your life.

*Mel.*　Quench me this mighty humour, and then tell me
　　　　Whose Whore you are, for you are one, I know it.
　　　　Let all mine honours perish but I'le find him,
　　　　Though he lie lockt up in thy blood; be sudden;
　　　　There is no facing it, and be not flattered;
　　　　The burnt air, when the *Dog* raigns, is not fouler
　　　　Than thy contagious name, till thy repentance
　　　　(If the Gods grant thee any) purge thy sickness.

*Evad.*　Be gone, you are my Brother, that's your safety.

*Mel.*　I'le be a Wolf first; 'tis to be thy Brother
　　　　An infamy below the sin of a Coward:
　　　　I am as far from being part of thee,
　　　　As thou art from thy vertue: seek a kindred
　　　　Mongst sensual beasts, and make a Goat thy Brother,
　　　　A Goat is cooler; will you tell me yet?

*Evad.*　If you stay here and rail thus, I shall tell you,
　　　　I'le ha' you whipt; get you to your command,
　　　　And there preach to your Sentinels,
　　　　And tell them what a brave man you are; I shall laugh at
　　　　you.

*Mel.*　Y'are grown a glorious Whore; where be your daring,
　　　　And I alive? by my just Sword, h'ad safer
　　　　Bestride a Billow when the angry North

59

Plows up the Sea, or made Heavens fire his food;
Work me no higher; will you discover yet?

*Evad.*    The Fellow's mad, sleep and speak sense.

*Mel.*    Force my swollen heart no further; I would save
thee; your great maintainers are not here, they dare
not, would they were all, and armed, I would speak
loud; here's one should thunder to 'em: will you tell
me? thou hast no hope to scape; he that dares most,
and damns away his soul to do thee service, will
sooner fetch meat from a hungry Lion, than come to
rescue thee; thou hast death about thee: h'as
undone thine honour, poyson'd thy vertue, and of a
lovely rose, left thee a canker.

*Evad.*    Let me consider.

*Mel.*    Do, whose child thou wert,
Whose honour thou hast murdered, whose grave open'd,
And so pull'd on the Gods, that in their justice
They must restore him flesh again and life,
And raise his dry bones to revenge his scandal.

*Evad.*    The gods are not of my mind; they had better let 'em lie
sweet still in the earth; they'l stink here.

*Mel.*    Do you raise mirth out of my easiness?
Forsake me then all weaknesses of Nature,
That make men women: Speak you whore, speak truth,
Or by the dear soul of thy sleeping Father,
This sword shall be thy lover: tell, or I'le kill thee:
And when thou hast told all, thou wilt deserve it.

*Evad.*    You will not murder me!

*Mel.*    No, 'tis a justice, and a noble one,
To put the light out of such base offenders.

*Evad.*    Help!

*Mel.*    By thy foul self, no humane help shall help thee,
If thou criest: when I have kill'd thee, as I have

Vow'd to do, if thou confess not, naked as thou hast left
Thine honour, will I leave thee,
That on thy branded flesh the world may read
Thy black shame, and my justice; wilt thou bend yet?

*Evad.*   Yes.

*Mel.*   Up and begin your story.

*Evad.*   Oh I am miserable.

*Mel.*   'Tis true, thou art, speak truth still.

*Evad.*   I have offended, noble Sir: forgive me.

*Mel.*   With what secure slave?

*Evad.*   Do not ask me Sir.
    Mine own remembrance is a misery too mightie for me.

*Mel.*   Do not fall back again; my sword's unsheath'd yet.

*Evad.*   What shall I do?

*Mel.*   Be true, and make your fault less.

*Evad.*   I dare not tell.

*Mel.*   Tell, or I'le be this day a killing thee.

*Evad.*   Will you forgive me then?

*Mel.*   Stay, I must ask mine honour first, I have too much foolish
    nature in me; speak.

*Evad.*   Is there none else here?

*Mel.*   None but a fearful conscience, that's too many. Who is't?

*Evad.*   O hear me gently; it was the King.

*Mel.*   No more. My worthy father's and my services
    Are liberally rewarded! King, I thank thee,

For all my dangers and my wounds, thou hast paid me
In my own metal: These are Souldiers thanks.
How long have you liv'd thus *Evadne*?

*Evad.*    Too long.

*Mel.*    Too late you find it: can you be sorry?

*Evad.*    Would I were half as blameless.

*Mel.*    *Evadne*, thou wilt to thy trade again.

*Evad.*    First to my grave.

*Mel.*    Would gods th'hadst been so blest:
    Dost thou not hate this King now? prethee hate him:
    Couldst thou not curse him? I command thee curse him,
    Curse till the gods hear, and deliver him
    To thy just wishes: yet I fear *Evadne*;
    You had rather play your game out.

*Evad.*    No, I feel
    Too many sad confusions here to let in any loose flame
    hereafter.

*Mel.*    Dost thou not feel amongst all those one brave anger
    That breaks out nobly, and directs thine arm to kill this
    base King?

*Evad.*    All the gods forbid it.

*Mel.*    No, all the gods require it, they are dishonoured in him.

*Evad.*    'Tis too fearful.

*Mel.*    Y'are valiant in his bed, and bold enough
    To be a stale whore, and have your Madams name
    Discourse for Grooms and Pages, and hereafter
    When his cool Majestie hath laid you by,
    To be at pension with some needy Sir
    For meat and courser clothes, thus far you know no fear.
    Come, you shall kill him.

*Evad.*   Good Sir!

*Mel.*   And 'twere to kiss him dead, thou'd smother him;
        Be wise and kill him: Canst thou live and know
        What noble minds shall make thee see thy self
        Found out with every finger, made the shame
        Of all successions, and in this great ruine
        Thy brother and thy noble husband broken?
        Thou shalt not live thus; kneel and swear to help me
        When I shall call thee to it, or by all
        Holy in heaven and earth, thou shalt not live
        To breath a full hour longer, not a thought:
        Come 'tis a righteous oath; give me thy hand,
        And both to heaven held up, swear by that wealth
        This lustful thief stole from thee, when I say it,
        To let his foul soul out.

*Evad.*   Here I swear it,
        And all you spirits of abused Ladies
        Help me in this performance.

*Mel.*   Enough; this must be known to none
        But you and I *Evadne*; not to your Lord,
        Though he be wise and noble, and a fellow
        Dares step as far into a worthy action,
        As the most daring, I as far as Justice.
        Ask me not why. Farewell.

                    [*Exit Mel.*

*Evad.*   Would I could say so to my black disgrace.
        Oh where have I been all this time! how friended,
        That I should lose my self thus desperately,
        And none for pity shew me how I wandred?
        There is not in the compass of the light
        A more unhappy creature: sure I am monstrous,
        For I have done those follies, those mad mischiefs,
        Would dare a woman. O my loaden soul,
        Be not so cruel to me, choak not up

                    [*Enter Amintor.*

The way to my repentance. O my Lord.

*Amin.*   How now?

*Evad.*   My much abused Lord!

                    [*Kneels.*

*Amin.*   This cannot be.

*Evad.*   I do not kneel to live, I dare not hope it;
        The wrongs I did are greater; look upon me
        Though I appear with all my faults.

*Amin.*   Stand up.
        This is no new way to beget more sorrow;
        Heaven knows I have too many; do not mock me;
        Though I am tame and bred up with my wrongs,
        Which are my foster-brothers, I may leap
        Like a hand-wolf into my natural wilderness,
        And do an out-rage: pray thee do not mock me.

*Evad.*   My whole life is so leprous, it infects
        All my repentance: I would buy your pardon
        Though at the highest set, even with my life:
        That slight contrition, that's no sacrifice
        For what I have committed.

*Amin.*   Sure I dazle:
        There cannot be a faith in that foul woman
        That knows no God more mighty than her mischiefs:
        Thou dost still worst, still number on thy faults,
        To press my poor heart thus.  Can I believe
        There's any seed of Vertue in that woman
        Left to shoot up, that dares go on in sin
        Known, and so known as thine is, O *Evadne*!
        Would there were any safety in thy sex,
        That I might put a thousand sorrows off,
        And credit thy repentance: but I must not;
        Thou hast brought me to the dull calamity,
        To that strange misbelief of all the world,
        And all things that are in it, that I fear
        I shall fall like a tree, and find my grave,
        Only remembring that I grieve.

*Evad.*   My Lord,

Give me your griefs: you are an innocent,
A soul as white as heaven: let not my sins
Perish your noble youth: I do not fall here
To shadow by dissembling with my tears,
As all say women can, or to make less
What my hot will hath done, which heaven and you
Knows to be tougher than the hand of time
Can cut from mans remembrance; no I do not;
I do appear the same, the same *Evadne*,
Drest in the shames I liv'd in, the same monster.
But these are names of honour, to what I am;
I do present my self the foulest creature,
Most poysonous, dangerous, and despis'd of men,
*Lerna* e're bred, or *Nilus*; I am hell,
Till you, my dear Lord, shoot your light into me,
The beams of your forgiveness: I am soul-sick,
And [wither] with the fear of one condemn'd,
Till I have got your pardon.

*Amin.*   Rise *Evadne*,
Those heavenly powers that put this good into thee,
Grant a continuance of it: I forgive thee;
Make thy self worthy of it, and take heed,
Take heed *Evadne* this be serious;
Mock not the powers above, that can and dare
Give thee a great example of their justice
To all ensuing eyes, if thou plai'st
With thy repentance, the best sacrifice.

*Evad.*   I have done nothing good to win belief,
My life hath been so faithless; all the creatures
Made for heavens honours have their ends, and good ones,
All but the cousening *Crocodiles*, false women;
They reign here like those plagues, those killing sores
Men pray against; and when they die, like tales
Ill told, and unbeliev'd, they pass away,
And go to dust forgotten: But my Lord,
Those short dayes I shall number to my rest,
(As many must not see me) shall though too late,
Though in my evening, yet perceive a will,
Since I can do no good because a woman,
Reach constantly at some thing that is near it;
I will redeem one minute of my age,

Or like another *Niobe* I'le weep till I am water.

*Amin.*    I am now dissolved:
      My frozen soul melts: may each sin thou hast,
      Find a new mercy: Rise, I am at peace:
      Hadst thou been thus, thus excellently good,
      Before that devil King tempted thy frailty,
      Sure thou hadst made a star: give me thy hand;
      From this time I will know thee, and as far
      As honour gives me leave, be thy *Amintor*:
      When we meet next, I will salute thee fairly,
      And pray the gods to give thee happy dayes:
      My charity shall go along with thee,
      Though my embraces must be far from thee.
      I should ha' kill'd thee, but this sweet repentance
      Locks up my vengeance, for which thus I kiss thee,
      The last kiss we must take; and would to heaven
      The holy Priest that gave our hands together,
      Had given us equal Vertues: go *Evadne*,
      The gods thus part our bodies, have a care
      My honour falls no farther, I am well then.

*Evad.*    All the dear joyes here, and above hereafter
      Crown thy fair soul: thus I take leave my Lord,
      And never shall you see the foul *Evadne*
      Till sh'ave tryed all honoured means that may
      Set her in rest, and wash her stains away.

            [*Exeunt.*

*Banquet. Enter King, Calianax. Hoboyes play within.*

*King.*    I cannot tell how I should credit this
      From you that are his enemy.

*Cal.*    I am sure he said it to me, and I'le justifie it
      What way he dares oppose, but with my sword.

*King.*    But did he break without all circumstance
      To you his foe, that he would have the Fort
      To kill me, and then escape?

*Cal.*    If he deny it, I'le make him blush.

*King.*    It sounds incredibly.

*Cal.*    I, so does every thing I say of late.

*King.*    Not so *Calianax*.

*Cal.*    Yes, I should sit
Mute, whilst a Rogue with strong arms cuts your throat.

*King.*    Well, I will try him, and if this be true
I'le pawn my life I'le find it; if't be false,
And that you clothe your hate in such a lie,
You shall hereafter doat in your own house, not in the
Court.

*Cal.*    Why if it be a lie,
Mine ears are false; for I'le be sworn I heard it:
Old men are good for nothing; you were best
Put me to death for hearing, and free him
For meaning of it; you would ha' trusted me
Once, but the time is altered.

*King.*    And will still where I may do with justice to the world;
You have no witness.

*Cal.*    Yes, my self.

*King.*    No more I mean there were that heard it.

*Cal.*    How no more? would you have more? why am
Not I enough to hang a thousand Rogues?

*King.*    But so you may hang honest men too if you please.

*Cal.*    I may, 'tis like I will do so; there are a hundred will swear it
for a need too, if I say it.

*King.*    Such witnesses we need not.

*Cal.*    And 'tis hard if my Word cannot hang a boysterous knave.

*King.*    Enough; where's *Strato*?

*Stra.* Sir!

*Enter Strato.*

*King.* Why where's all the company? call *Amintor* in.
   *Evadne*, where's my Brother, and *Melantius*?
   Bid him come too, and *Diphilus*; call all

       *[Exit Strato.*

   That are without there: if he should desire
   The combat of you, 'tis not in the power
   Of all our Laws to hinder it, unless we mean to quit 'em.

*Cal.* Why if you do think
   'Tis fit an old Man and a Counsellor,
   To fight for what he sayes, then you may grant it.

*Enter Amin. Evad. Mel. Diph. [Lisip.] Cle. Stra. Diag.*

*King.* Come Sirs, *Amintor* thou art yet a Bridegroom,
   And I will use thee so: thou shalt sit down;
   *Evadne* sit, and you *Amintor* too;
   This Banquet is for you, sir: Who has brought
   A merry Tale about him, to raise a laughter
   Amongst our wine? why *Strato*, where art thou?
   Thou wilt chop out with them unseasonably
   When I desire 'em not.

*Strato.* 'Tis my ill luck Sir, so to spend them then.

*King.* Reach me a boul of wine: *Melantlius*, thou art sad.

*Amin.* I should be Sir the merriest here,
   But I ha' ne're a story of mine own
   Worth telling at this time.

*King.* Give me the Wine.
   *Melantius*, I am now considering
   How easie 'twere for any man we trust
   To poyson one of us in such a boul.

*Mel.* I think it were not hard Sir, for a Knave.

Cal.     Such as you are.

King.    I' faith 'twere easie, it becomes us well
         To get plain dealing men about our selves,
         Such as you all are here: *Amintor*, to thee
         And to thy fair *Evadne*.

Mel.     Have you thought of this *Calianax*?

                     [*Aside.*

Cal.     Yes marry have I.

Mel.     And what's your resolution?

Cal.     Ye shall have it soundly?

King.    Reach to *Amintor*, *Strato*.

Amin.    Here my love,
         This Wine will do thee wrong, for it will set
         Blushes upon thy cheeks, and till thou dost a
         fault, 'twere pity.

King.    Yet I wonder much
         Of the strange desperation of these men,
         That dare attempt such acts here in our State;
         He could not escape that did it.

Mel.     Were he known, unpossible.

King.    It would be known, *Melantius*.

Mel.     It ought to be, if he got then away
         He must wear all our lives upon his sword,
         He need not fly the Island, he must leave no one alive.

King.    No, I should think no man
         Could kill me and scape clear, but that old man.

Cal.     But I! heaven bless me: I, should I my Liege?

King.    I do not think thou wouldst, but yet thou might'st,

For thou hast in thy hands the means to scape,
By keeping of the Fort; he has, *Melantius*, and he has
kept it well.

*Mel.*  From cobwebs Sir,
'Tis clean swept: I can find no other Art
In keeping of it now, 'twas ne're besieg'd since he
commanded.

*Cal.*  I shall be sure of your good word,
But I have kept it safe from such as you.

*Mel.*  Keep your ill temper in,
I speak no malice; had my brother kept it I should ha' said
as much.

*King.*  You are not merry, brother; drink wine,
Sit you all still! *Calianax,*      [*Aside.*
I cannot trust thus: I have thrown out words
That would have fetcht warm blood upon the cheeks
Of guilty men, and he is never mov'd, he knows no such
thing.

*Cal.*  Impudence may scape, when feeble vertue is accus'd.

*King.*  He must, if he were guilty, feel an alteration
At this our whisper, whilst we point at him,
You see he does not.

*Cal.*  Let him hang himself,
What care I what he does; this he did say.

*King.*  *Melantius*, you cannot easily conceive
What I have meant; for men that are in fault
Can subtly apprehend when others aime
At what they do amiss; but I forgive
Freely before this man; heaven do so too:
I will not touch thee so much as with shame
Of telling it, let it be so no more.

*Cal.*  Why this is very fine.

*Mel.*  I cannot tell

What 'tis you mean, but I am apt enough
Rudely to thrust into ignorant fault,
But let me know it; happily 'tis nought
But misconstruction, and where I am clear
I will not take forgiveness of the gods, much less of you.

*King.*  Nay if you stand so stiff, I shall call back my mercy.

*Mel.*  I want smoothness
    To thank a man for pardoning of a crime I never knew.

*King.*  Not to instruct your knowledge, but to shew you
    my ears are every where, you meant to kill me, and get
    the Fort to scape.

*Mel.*  Pardon me Sir; my bluntness will be pardoned:
    You preserve
    A race of idle people here about you,
    Eaters, and talkers, to defame the worth
    Of those that do things worthy; the man that uttered this
    Had perisht without food, be't who it will,
    But for this arm that fenc't him from the foe.
    And if I thought you gave a faith to this,
    The plainness of my nature would speak more;
    Give me a pardon (for you ought to do't)
    To kill him that spake this.

*Cal.*  I, that will be the end of all,
    Then I am fairly paid for all my care and service.

*Mel.*  That old man who calls me enemy, and of whom I
    (Though I will never match my hate so low)
    Have no good thought, would yet I think excuse me,
    And swear he thought me wrong'd in this.

*Cal.*  Who I, thou shameless fellow! didst thou not speak to me of
    it thy self?

*Mel.*  O then it came from him.

*Cal.*  From me! who should it come from but from me?

*Mel.*  Nay, I believe your malice is enough,

But I ha' lost my anger. Sir, I hope you are well satisfied.

| | |
|---|---|
| *King.* | *Lisip.* Chear *Amintor* and his Lady; there's no sound<br>Comes from you; I will come and do't my self. |

| | |
|---|---|
| *Amin.* | You have done already Sir for me, I thank you. |

| | |
|---|---|
| *King.* | *Melantius*, I do credit this from him,<br>How slight so e're you mak't. |

| | |
|---|---|
| *Mel.* | 'Tis strange you should. |

| | |
|---|---|
| *Cal.* | 'Tis strange he should believe an old mans word,<br>That never lied in his life. |

| | |
|---|---|
| *Mel.* | I talk not to thee;<br>Shall the wild words of this distempered man,<br>Frantick with age and sorrow, make a breach<br>Betwixt your Majesty and me? 'twas wrong<br>To hearken to him; but to credit him<br>As much, at least, as I have power to bear.<br>But pardon me, whilst I speak only truth,<br>I may commend my self—I have bestow'd<br>My careless blood with you, and should be loth<br>To think an action that would make me lose<br>That, and my thanks too: when I was a boy,<br>I thrust my self into my Countries cause,<br>And did a deed that pluckt five years from time,<br>And stil'd me man then: And for you my King,<br>Your subjects all have fed by vertue of my arm.<br>This sword of mine hath plow'd the ground,<br>And reapt the fruit in peace;<br>And your self have liv'd at home in ease:<br>So terrible I grew, that without swords<br>My name hath fetcht you conquest, and my heart<br>And limbs are still the same; my will is great<br>To do you service: let me not be paid<br>With such a strange distrust. |

| | |
|---|---|
| *King.* | *Melantius*, I held it great injustice to believe<br>Thine Enemy, and did not; if I did,<br>I do not, let that satisfie: what struck<br>With sadness all? More Wine! |

The Maids Tragedy

*Cal.*    A few fine words have overthrown my truth:
        Ah th'art a Villain.

*Mel.*    Why thou wert better let me have the Fort,
        Dotard, I will disgrace thee thus for ever;

                [*Aside.*

        There shall no credit lie upon thy words;
        Think better and deliver it.

*Cal.*    My Liege, he's at me now agen to do it; speak,
        Deny it if thou canst; examine him
        Whilst he's hot, for he'l cool agen, he will forswear it.

*King.*    This is lunacy I hope, *Melantius.*

*Mel.*    He hath lost himself
        Much since his Daughter mist the happiness
        My Sister gain'd; and though he call me Foe, I pity him.

*Cal.*    Pity! a pox upon you.

*King.*    Mark his disordered words, and at the Mask.

*Mel.*    *Diagoras* knows he raged, and rail'd at me,
        And cal'd a Lady Whore, so innocent
        She understood him not; but it becomes
        Both you and me too, to forgive distraction,
        Pardon him as I do.

*Cal.*    I'le not speak for thee, for all thy cunning, if you
        will be safe chop off his head, for there was never
        known so impudent a Rascal.

*King.*    Some that love him, get him to bed: Why, pity
        should not let age make it self contemptible; we must
        be all old, have him away.

*Mel.*    *Calianax,* the King believes you; come, you shall go
        Home, and rest; you ha' done well; you'l give it up
        When I have us'd you thus a moneth I hope.

*Cal.*     Now, now, 'tis plain Sir, he does move me still;
        He sayes he knows I'le give him up the Fort,
        When he has us'd me thus a moneth: I am mad,
        Am I not still?

*Omnes.*   Ha, ha, ha!

*Cal.*     I shall be mad indeed, if you do thus;
        Why would you trust a sturdy fellow there
        (That has no vertue in him, all's in his sword)
        Before me? do but take his weapons from him,
        And he's an Ass, and I am a very fool,
        Both with him, and without him, as you use me.

*Omnes.*   Ha, ha, ha!

*King.*    'Tis well *Calianax*; but if you use
        This once again, I shall intreat some other
        To see your Offices be well discharg'd.
        Be merry Gentlemen, it grows somewhat late.
        *Amintor*, thou wouldest be abed again.

*Amin.*   Yes Sir.

*King.*    And you *Evadne*; let me take thee in my arms,
        *Melantius*, and believe thou art as thou deservest to
        be, my friend still, and for ever. Good *Calianax*,
        Sleep soundly, it will bring thee to thy self.

              [*Exeunt omnes. Manent Mel. and Cal.*

*Cal.*     Sleep soundly! I sleep soundly now I hope,
        I could not be thus else. How dar'st thou stay
        Alone with me, knowing how thou hast used me?

*Mel.*    You cannot blast me with your tongue,
        And that's the strongest part you have about you.

*Cal.*     I do look for some great punishment for this,
        For I begin to forget all my hate,
        And tak't unkindly that mine enemy
        Should use me so extraordinarily scurvily.

*Mel.*    I shall melt too, if you begin to take
        Unkindnesses: I never meant you hurt.

*Cal.*    Thou'lt anger me again; thou wretched rogue,
        Meant me no hurt! disgrace me with the King;
        Lose all my Offices! this is no hurt,
        Is it? I prethee what dost thou call hurt?

*Mel.*    To poyson men because they love me not;
        To call the credit of mens Wives in question;
        To murder children betwixt me and land; this is all hurt.

*Cal.*    All this thou think'st is sport;
        For mine is worse: but use thy will with me;
        For betwixt grief and anger I could cry.

*Mel.*    Be wise then, and be safe; thou may'st revenge.

*Cal.*    I o'th' King? I would revenge of thee.

*Mel.*    That you must plot your self.

*Cal.*    I am a fine plotter.

*Mel.*    The short is, I will hold thee with the King
        In this perplexity, till peevishness
        And thy disgrace have laid thee in thy grave:
        But if thou wilt deliver up the Fort,
        I'le take thy trembling body in my arms,
        And bear thee over dangers; thou shalt hold thy wonted
        state.

*Cal.*    If I should tell the King, can'st thou deny't again?

*Mel.*    Try and believe.

*Cal.*    Nay then, thou can'st bring any thing about:
        Thou shalt have the Fort.

*Mel.*    Why well, here let our hate be buried, and
        This hand shall right us both; give me thy aged breast to
        compass.

Cal.    Nay, I do not love thee yet:
       I cannot well endure to look on thee:
       And if I thought it were a courtesie,
       Thou should'st not have it: but I am disgrac'd;
       My Offices are to be ta'ne away;
       And if I did but hold this Fort a day,
       I do believe the King would take it from me,
       And give it thee, things are so strangely carried;
       Nere thank me for't; but yet the King shall know
       There was some such thing in't I told him of;
       And that I was an honest man.

Mel.    Hee'l buy that knowledge very dearly.

[*Enter Diphilus.*

       What news with thee?

Diph.    This were a night indeed to do it in;
       The King hath sent for her.

Mel.    She shall perform it then; go *Diphilus*,
       And take from this good man, my worthy friend,
       The Fort; he'l give it thee.

Diph.    Ha' you got that?

Cal.    Art thou of the same breed? canst thou deny
       This to the King too?

Diph.    With a confidence as great as his.

Cal.    Faith, like enough.

Mel.    Away, and use him kindly.

Cal.    Touch not me, I hate the whole strain: if thou follow me a
       great way off, I'le give thee up the
       Fort; and hang your selves.

Mel.    Be gone.

Diph.    He's finely wrought.

*[Exeunt Cal. Diph.*

*Mel.*     This is a night in spite of Astronomers
        To do the deed in; I will wash the stain
        That rests upon our House, off with his blood.

*Enter Amintor.*

*Amin.*    *Melantius,* now assist me if thou beest
        That which thou say'st, assist me: I have lost
        All my distempers, and have found a rage so pleasing;
        help me.

*Mel.*     Who can see him thus,
        And not swear vengeance? what's the matter friend?

*Amin.*    Out with thy sword; and hand in hand with me
        Rush to the Chamber of this hated King,
        And sink him with the weight of all his sins to hell for
        ever.

*Mel.*     'Twere a rash attempt,
        Not to be done with safety: let your reason
        Plot your revenge, and not your passion.

*Amint.*   If thou refusest me in these extreams,
        Thou art no friend: he sent for her to me;
        By Heaven to me; my self; and I must tell ye
        I love her as a stranger; there is worth
        In that vile woman, worthy things, *Melantius;*
        And she repents. I'le do't my self alone,
        Though I be slain. Farewell.

*Mel.*     He'l overthrow my whole design with madness:
        *Amintor,* think what thou doest; I dare as much as valour;
        But 'tis the King, the King, the King, *Amintor,*
        With whom thou fightest; I know he's honest,

*[Aside.*

        And this will work with him.

*Amint.*   I cannot tell

What thou hast said; but thou hast charm'd my sword
Out of my hand, and left me shaking here defenceless.

*Mel.* I will take it up for thee.

*Amint.* What a wild beast is uncollected man!
  The thing that we call Honour, bears us all
  Headlong unto sin, and yet it self is nothing.

*Mel.* Alas, how variable are thy thoughts!

*Amint.* Just like my fortunes: I was run to that
  I purpos'd to have chid thee for.
  Some Plot I did distrust thou hadst against the King
  By that old fellows carriage: but take heed,
  There is not the least limb growing to a King,
  But carries thunder in it.

*Mel.* I have none against him.

*Amint.* Why, come then, and still remember we may not think
  revenge.

*Mel.* I will remember.

# The Maids Tragedy

*Actus Quintus.*

*Enter* Evadne *and a* Gentleman.

*Evad.*   Sir, is the King abed?

*Gent.*   Madam, an hour ago.

*Evad.*   Give me the key then, and let none be near;
          'Tis the Kings pleasure.

*Gent.*   I understand you Madam, would 'twere mine.
          I must not wish good rest unto your Ladiship.

*Evad.*   You talk, you talk.

*Gent.*  'Tis all I dare do, Madam; but the King will wake, and then.

*Evad.*   Saving your imagination, pray good night Sir.

*Gent.*   A good night be it then, and a long one Madam;
          I am gone.

*Evad.*   The night grows horrible, and all about me
          Like my black purpose: O the Conscience
                              [*King abed.*

          Of a lost Virgin; whither wilt thou pull me?
          To what things dismal, as the depth of Hell,
          Wilt thou provoke me? Let no [woman] dare
          From this hour be disloyal: if her heart
          Be flesh, if she have blood, and can fear, 'tis a daring
          Above that desperate fool that left his peace,
          And went to Sea to fight: 'tis so many sins
          An age cannot prevent 'em: and so great,
          The gods want mercy for: yet I must through 'em.
          I have begun a slaughter on my honour,
          And I must end it there: he sleeps, good heavens!
          Why give you peace to this untemperate beast
          That hath so long transgressed you? I must kill him,
          And I will do't bravely: the meer joy
          Tells me I merit in it: yet I must not

79

Thus tamely do it as he sleeps: that were
To rock him to another world: my vengeance
Shall take him waking, and then lay before him
The number of his wrongs and punishments.
I'le shake his sins like furies, till I waken
His evil Angel, his sick Conscience:
And then I'le strike him dead: King, by your leave:

[*Ties his armes to the bed.*

I dare not trust your strength: your Grace and I
Must grapple upon even terms no more:
So, if he rail me not from my resolution,
I shall be strong enough.
My Lord the King, my Lord; he sleeps
As if he meant to wake no more, my Lord;
Is he not dead already? Sir, my Lord.

*King.*    Who's that?

*Evad.*    O you sleep soundly Sir!

*King.*    My dear *Evadne,*
       I have been dreaming of thee; come to bed.

*Evad.*    I am come at length Sir, but how welcome?

*King.*    What pretty new device is this *Evadne*?
       What do you tie me to you by my love?
       This is a quaint one: Come my dear and kiss me;
       I'le be thy *Mars* to bed my Queen of Love:
       Let us be caught together, that the Gods may see,
       And envy our embraces.

*Evad.*    Stay Sir, stay,
       You are too hot, and I have brought you Physick
       To temper your high veins.

*King.*    Prethee to bed then; let me take it warm,
       There you shall know the state of my body better.

*Evad.*    I know you have a surfeited foul body,
       And you must bleed.

The Maids Tragedy

*King.* Bleed!

*Evad.* I, you shall bleed: lie still, and if the Devil,
Your lust will give you leave, repent: this steel
Comes to redeem the honour that you stole,
King, my fair name, which nothing but thy death
Can answer to the world.

*King.* How's this *Evadne*?

*Evad.* I am not she: nor bear I in this breast
So much cold Spirit to be call'd a Woman:
I am a Tyger: I am any thing
That knows not pity: stir not, if thou dost,
I'le take thee unprepar'd; thy fears upon thee,
That make thy sins look double, and so send thee
(By my revenge I will) to look those torments
Prepar'd for such black souls.

*King.* Thou dost not mean this: 'tis impossible:
Thou art too sweet and gentle.

*Evad.* No, I am not:
I am as foul as thou art, and can number
As many such hells here: I was once fair,
Once I was lovely, not a blowing Rose
More chastly sweet, till tho[u], thou, thou, foul
Canker,
(Stir not) didst poyson me: I was a world of vertue,
Till your curst Court and you (hell bless you for't)
With your temptations on temptations
Made me give up mine honour; for which (King)
I am come to kill thee.

*King.* No.

*Evad.* I am.

*King.* Thou art not.
I prethee speak not these things; thou art gentle,
And wert not meant thus rugged.

81

*Evad.*    Peace and hear me.
    Stir nothing but your tongue, and that for mercy
    To those above us; by whose lights I vow,
    Those blessed fires that shot to see our sin,
    If thy hot soul had substance with thy blood,
    I would kill that too, which being past my steel,
    My tongue shall teach: Thou art a shameless Villain,
    A thing out of the overchange of Nature;
    Sent like a thick cloud to disperse a plague
    Upon weak catching women; such a tyrant
    That for his Lust would sell away his Subjects,
    I, all his heaven hereafter.

*King.*    Hear *Evadne*,
    Thou soul of sweetness! hear, I am thy King.

*Evad.*    Thou art my shame; lie still, there's none about you,
    Within your cries; all promises of safety
    Are but deluding dreams: thus, thus, thou foul man,
    Thus I begin my vengeance.

        [*Stabs him.*

*King.*    Hold *Evadne*!
    I do command thee hold.

*Evad.*    I do not mean Sir,
    To part so fairly with you; we must change
    More of these love-tricks yet.

*King.*    What bloody villain
    Provok't thee to this murther?

*Evad.*    Thou, thou monster.

*King.*    Oh!

*Evad.*    Thou kept'st me brave at Court, and Whor'd me;
    Then married me to a young noble Gentleman;
    And Whor'd me still.

*King.*    *Evadne*, pity me.

The Maids Tragedy

*Evad.*    Hell take me then; this for my Lord *Amintor*;
          This for my noble brother: and this stroke
          For the most wrong'd of women.

                   [*Kills him.*

*King.*    Oh! I die.

*Evad.*    Die all our faults together; I forgive thee.

                   [*Exit.*

*Enter two of the Bed-Chamber.*

1.       Come now she's gone, let's enter, the King expects it, and
         will be angry.

2.       'Tis a fine wench, we'l have a snap at her one of these nights
         as she goes from him.

1.       Content: how quickly he had done with her! I see
         Kings can do no more that way than other mortal people.

2.       How fast he is! I cannot hear him breathe.

1.       Either the Tapers give a feeble light, or he looks very  pale.

2.       And so he does, pray Heaven he be well.
         Let's look: Alas! he's stiffe, wounded and dead:
         Treason, Treason!

1.       Run forth and call.

                 [*Exit Gent.*

2.       Treason, Treason!

1.       This will be laid on us: who can believe
         A Woman could do this?

*Enter* Cleon *and* Lisippus.

*Cleon.*   How now, where's the Traytor?

1.  Fled, fled away; but there her woful act lies still.

*Cle.* Her act! a Woman!

*Lis.* Where's the body?

1.  There.

*Lis.* Farewel thou worthy man; there were two bonds
   That tyed our loves, a Brother and a King;
   The least of which might fetch a flood of tears:
   But such the misery of greatness is,
   They have no time to mourn; then pardon me.
   Sirs, which way went she?

       [*Enter Strato.*

*Strat.* Never follow her,
   For she alas! was but the instrument.
   News is now brought in, that *Melantius*
   Has got the Fort, and stands upon the wall;
   And with a loud voice calls those few that pass
   At this dead time of night, delivering
   The innocent of this act.

*Lis.* Gentlemen, I am your King.

*Strat.* We do acknowledge it.

*Lis.* I would I were not: follow all; for this must have a sudden
  stop.

       [*Exeunt*

*Enter* Melant. Diph. *and* Cal. *on the wall.*

*Mel.* If the dull people can believe I am arm'd,
   Be constant *Diphilus*; now we have time,
   Either to bring our banisht honours home,
   Or create new ones in our ends.

*Diph.* I fear not;
   My spirit lies not that way. Courage *Calianax.*

*Cal.*    Would I had any, you should quickly know it.

*Mel.*    Speak to the people; thou art eloquent.

*Cal.*    'Tis a fine eloquence to come to the gallows;
            You were born to be my end; the Devil take you.
            Now must I hang for company; 'tis strange
            I should be old, and neither wise nor valiant.

    *Enter* Lisip. Diag. Cleon, Strat. Guard.

*Lisip.*  See where he stands as boldly confident,
            As if he had his full command about him.

*Strat.*  He looks as if he had the bet[t]er cause; Sir,
            Under your gracious pardon let me speak it;
            Though he be mighty-spirited and forward
            To all great things; to all things of that danger
            Worse men shake at the telling of; yet certainly
            I do believe him noble, and this action
            Rather pull'd on than sought; his mind was ever
            As worthy as his hand.

*Lis.*    'Tis my fear too;
            Heaven forgive all: summon him Lord *Cleon.*

*Cleon.*  Ho from the walls there.

*Mel.*    Worthy *Cleon*, welcome;
            We could have wisht you here Lord; you are honest.

*Cal.*    Well, thou art as flattering a knave, though I dare not tell you
              so.

                    [*Aside.*

*Lis.*    *Melantius!*

*Mel.*    Sir.

*Lis.*    I am sorry that we meet thus; our old love
            Never requir'd such distance; pray Heaven
            You have not left your self, and sought this safety

More out of fear than honour; you have lost
A noble Master, which your faith *Melantius*,
Some think might have preserv'd; yet you know best.

*Cal.*      When time was I was mad; some that dares
Fight I hope will pay this Rascal.

*Mel.*      Royal young man, whose tears look lovely on thee;
Had they been shed for a deserving one,
They had been lasting monuments. Thy Brother,
Whil'st he was good, I call'd him King, and serv'd him
With that strong faith, that most unwearied valour;
Pul'd people from the farthest Sun to seek him;
And by his friendship, I was then his souldier;
But since his hot pride drew him to disgrace me,
And brand my noble actions with his lust,
(That never cur'd dishonour of my Sister,
Base stain of Whore; and which is worse,
The joy to make it still so) like my self;
Thus have I flung him off with my allegiance,
And stand here mine own justice to revenge
What I have suffered in him; and this old man
Wrong'd almost to lunacy.

*Cal.*      Who I? you'd draw me in: I have had no wrong,
I do disclaim ye all.

*Mel.*      The short is this;
'Tis no ambition to lift up my self,
Urgeth me thus; I do desire again
To be a subject, so I may be freed;
If not, I know my strength, and will unbuild
This goodly Town; be speedy, and be wise, in a reply.

*Strat.*      Be sudden Sir to tie
All again; what's done is past recal,
And past you to revenge; and there are thousands
That wait for such a troubled hour as this;
Throw him the blank.

*Lis.*      *Melantius*, write in that thy choice,
My Seal is at it.

*Mel.*    It was our honour drew us to this act,
          Not gain; and we will only work our pardon.

*Cal.*    Put my name in too.

*Diph.*   You disclaim'd us but now, *Calianax.*

*Cal.*    That's all one;
          I'le not be hanged hereafter by a trick;
          I'le have it in.

*Mel.*    You shall, you shall;
          Come to the back gate, and we'l call you King,
          And give you up the Fort.

*Lis.*    Away, away.

                    [*Exeunt Omnes.*

*Enter* Aspatia *in mans apparel.*

*Asp.*    This is my fatal hour; heaven may forgive
          My rash attempt, that causelesly hath laid
          Griefs on me that will never let me rest:
          And put a Womans heart into my brest;
          It is more honour for you that I die;
          For she that can endure the misery
          That I have on me, and be patient too,
          May live, and laugh at all that you can do.
          God save you Sir.
                    [*Enter Servant.*

*Ser.*    And you Sir; what's your business?

*Asp.*    With you Sir now, to do me the Office
          To help me to you[r] Lord.

*Ser.*    What, would you serve him?

*Asp.*    I'le do him any service; but to haste,
          For my affairs are earnest, I desire to speak with him.

*Ser.*    Sir, because you are in such haste, I would be loth delay you
          any longer: you cannot.

*Asp.*    It shall become you tho' to tell your Lord.

*Ser.*    Sir, he will speak with no body.

*Asp.*    This is most strange: art thou gold proof? there's for thee;
          help me to him.

*Ser.*    Pray be not angry Sir, I'le do my best.

                              [*Exit.*

*Asp.*    How stubbornly this fellow answer'd me!
          There is a vile dishonest trick in man,
          More than in women: all the men I meet
          Appear thus to me, are harsh and rude,
          And have a subtilty in every thing,
          Which love could never know; but we fond women
          Harbor the easiest and smoothest thoughts,
          And think all shall go so; it is unjust
          That men and women should be matcht together.

*Enter* Amintor *and his man.*

*Amint.*  Where is he!

*Ser.*    There my Lord.

*Amint.*  What would you Sir?

*Asp.*    Please it your Lordship to command your man
          Out of the room; shall deliver things
          Worthy your hearing.

*Amint.*  Leave us.

*Asp.*    O that that shape should bury falshood in it.

                              [*Aside.*

*Amint.*  Now your will Sir.

*Asp.*    When you know me, my Lord, you needs must guess
       My business! and I am not hard to know;
       For till the change of War mark'd this smooth face
       With these few blemishes people would call me
       My Sisters Picture, and her mine; in short,
       I am the brother to the wrong'd *Aspatia*.

*Amint.*   The wrong'd *Aspatia!* would thou wert so too
       Unto the wrong'd *Amintor*; let me kiss
       That hand of thine in honour that I bear
       Unto the wrong'd *Aspatia*: here I stand
       That did it; would he could not; gentle youth
       Leave me, for there is something in thy looks
       That calls my sins in a most hideous form
       Into my mind; and I have grief enough
       Without thy help.

*Asp.*    I would I could with credit:
       Since I was twelve years old I had not seen
       My Sister till this hour; I now arriv'd;
       She sent for me to see her Marriage,
       A woful one: but they that are above,
       Have ends in every thing; she us'd few words,
       But yet enough to make me understand
       The baseness of the injury you did her.
       That little training I have had is War;
       I may behave my self rudely in Peace;
       I would not though; I shall not need to tell you
       I am but young; and you would be loth to lose
       Honour that is not easily gain'd again.
       Fairly I mean to deal; the age is strict
       For single combats, and we shall be stopt
       If it be publish't: if you like your sword,
       Use it; if mine appear a better to you,
       Change; for the ground is this, and this the time
       To end our difference.

*Amint.*   Charitable youth,
       If thou be'st such, think not I will maintain
       So strange a wrong; and for thy Sisters sake,
       Know that I could not think that desperate thing
       I durst not do; yet to enjoy this world
       I would not see her; for beholding thee,

I am I know not what; if I have ought
That may content thee, take it and be gone;
For death is not so terrible as thou;
Thine eyes shoot guilt into me.

*Asp.*     Thus she swore
Thou would'st behave thy self, and give me words
That would fetch tears into mine eyes, and so
Thou dost indeed; but yet she bade me watch,
Lest I were cousen'd, and be sure to fight ere I return'd.

*Amint.*   That must not be with me;
For her I'le die directly, but against her will never hazard
it.

*Asp.*     You must be urg'd; I do not deal uncivilly with those that
Dare to fight; but such a one as you
Must be us'd thus.

                    *[She strikes him.*

*Amint.*   Prethee youth take heed;
Thy Sister is a thing to me so much
Above mine honour, that I can endu[r]e
All this; good gods—a blow I can endure;
But stay not, lest thou draw a timely death upon thy self.

*Asp.*     Thou art some prating fellow,
One that hath studyed out a trick to talk
And move soft-hearted people; to be kickt,

                    *[She kicks him.*

Thus to be kickt—why should he be so slow
                  *[Aside.*
In giving me my death?

*Amint.*   A man can bear
No more and keep his flesh; forgive me then;
I would endure yet if I could; now shew
The spirit thou pretendest, and understand
Thou hast no honour to live:

[*They fight.*

What dost thou mean? thou canst not fight:
The blows thou mak'st at me are quite besides;
And those I offer at thee, thou spread'st thine arms,
And tak'st upon thy breast, Alas! defenceless.

*Asp.*   I have got enough,
     And my desire; there's no place so fit for me to die as here.

*Enter* Evadne.

*Evad.*   *Amintor*; I am loaden with events
     That flie to make thee happy; I have joyes

[*Her hands bloody with a knife.*

     That in a moment can call back thy wrongs,
     And settle thee in thy free state again;
     It is *Evadne* still that follows thee, but not her
     mischiefs.

*Amint.*   Thou canst not fool me to believe agen;
     But thou hast looks and things so full of news that
     I am staid.

*Evad.*   Noble *Amintor*, put off thy amaze;
     Let thine eyes loose, and speak, am I not fair?
     Looks not *Evadne* beauteous with these rites now?
     Were those hours half so lovely in thine eyes,
     When our hands met before the holy man?
     I was too foul within to look fair then;
     Since I knew ill, I was not free till now.

*Amint.*   There is presage of some important thing
     About thee, which it seems thy tongue hath lost:
     Thy hands are bloody, and thou hast a knife.

*Evad.*   In this consists thy happiness and mine;
     Joy to *Amintor*, for the King is dead.

*Amint.*   Those have most power to hurt us that we love,
     We lay our sleeping lives within their arms.

Why, thou hast rais'd up mischief to this height,
And found out one to out-name thy other faults;
Thou hast no intermission of thy sins,
But all thy life is a continual ill;
Black is thy colour now, disease thy nature.
Joy to *Amintor*! thou hast toucht a life,
The very name of which had power to chain
Up all my rage, and calm my wildest wrongs.

*Evad.*   'Tis done; and since I could not find a way
To meet thy love so clear, as through his life,
I cannot now repent it.

*Amint.*   Could'st thou procure the Gods to speak to me,
To bid me love this woman, and forgive,
I think I should fall out with them; behold
Here lies a youth whose wounds bleed in my brest,
Sent by his violent Fate to fetch his death
From my slow hand: and to augment my woe,
You now are present stain'd with a Kings blood
Violently shed: this keeps night here,
And throws an unknown wilderness about me.

*Asp.*   Oh, oh, oh!

*Amint.*   No more, pursue me not.

*Evad.*   Forgive me then, and take me to thy bed.
We may not part.

*Amint.*   Forbear, be wise, and let my rage go this way.

*Evad.*   'Tis you that I would stay, not it.

*Amint.*   Take heed, it will return with me.

*Evad.*   If it must be, I shall not fear to meet it; take me home.

*Amint.*   Thou monster of cruelty, forbear.

*Evad.*   For heavens sake look more calm;
Thine eyes are sharper than thou canst make thy sword.

The Maids Tragedy

*Amint.*  Away, away, thy knees are more to me than violence.
I am worse than sick to see knees follow me
For that I must not grant; for heavens sake stand.

*Evad.*  Receive me then.*Amint.*   I dare not stay thy language;
In midst of all my anger and my grief,
Thou dost awake something that troubles me,
And sayes I lov'd thee once; I dare not stay;
There is no end of womens reasoning.

          *[Leaves her.*

*Evad.*  *Amintor*, thou shalt love me once again;
Go, I am calm; farewell; and peace for ever.
*Evadne* whom thou hat'st will die for thee.

          *[Kills her self.*

*Amint.*  I have a little humane nature yet
That's left for thee, that bids me stay thy hand.
          *[Returns.*

*Evad.*  Thy hand was welcome, but came too late;
Oh I am lost! the heavy sleep makes haste.

          *[She dies.*

*Asp.*  Oh, oh, oh!

*Amint.*  This earth of mine doth tremble, and I feel
A stark affrighted motion in my blood;
My soul grows weary of her house, and I
All over am a trouble to my self;
There is some hidden power in these dead things
That calls my flesh into'em; I am cold;
Be resolute, and bear'em company:
There's something yet which I am loth to leave.
There's man enough in me to meet the fears
That death can bring, and yet would it were done;
I can find nothing in the whole discourse
Of death, I durst not meet the boldest way;
Yet still betwixt the reason and the act,
The wrong I to *Aspatia* did stands up,

93

<blockquote>
I have not such a fault to answer,<br>
Though she may justly arm with scorn<br>
And hate of me, my soul will part less troubled,<br>
When I have paid to her in tears my sorrow:<br>
I will not leave this act unsatisfied,<br>
If all that's left in me can answer it.
</blockquote>

*Asp.* Was it a dream? there stands *Amintor* still:
Or I dream still.

*Amint.* How dost thou? speak, receive my love, and help:
Thy blood climbs up to his old place again:
There's hope of thy recovery.

*Asp.* Did you not name *Aspatia*?

*Amint.* I did.

*Asp.* And talkt of tears and sorrow unto her?

*Amint.* 'Tis true, and till these happy signs in thee
Did stay my course, 'twas thither I was going.

*Asp.* Th'art there already, and these wounds are hers:
Those threats I brought with me, sought not revenge,
But came to fetch this blessing from thy hand,
I am *Aspatia* yet.

*Amint.* Dare my soul ever look abroad agen?

*Asp.* I shall live *Amintor*; I am well:
A kind of healthful joy wanders within me.

*Amint.* The world wants lines to excuse thy loss:
Come let me bear thee to some place of help.

*Asp.* *Amintor* thou must stay, I must rest here,
My strength begins to disobey my will.
How dost thou my best soul? I would fain live,
Now if I could: would'st thou have loved me then?

*Amint.* Alas! all that I am's not worth a hair from thee.

*Asp.*    Give me thy hand, mine hands grope up and down,
          And cannot find thee; I am wondrous sick:
          Have I thy hand *Amintor*?
*Amint.*  Thou greatest blessing of the world, thou hast.

*Asp.*    I do believe thee better than my sense.
          Oh! I must go, farewell.

*Amint.*  She swounds: *Aspatia* help, for Heavens sake water;
          Such as may chain life for ever to this frame.
          *Aspatia*, speak: what no help? yet I fool,
          I'le chafe her temples, yet there's nothing stirs;
          Some hidden Power tell her that *Amintor* calls,
          And let her answer me: *Aspatia*, speak.
          I have heard, if there be life, but bow
          The body thus, and it will shew it self.
          Oh she is gone! I will not leave her yet.
          Since out of justice we must challenge nothing;
          I'le call it mercy if you'l pity me,
          You heavenly powers, and lend for some few years,
          The blessed soul to this fair seat agen.
          No comfort comes, the gods deny me too.
          I'le bow the body once agen: *Aspatia*!
          The soul is fled for ever, and I wrong
          My self, so long to lose her company.
          Must I talk now? Here's to be with thee love.

                    [*Kills himself.*

*Enter* Servant.

*Ser.*    This is a great grace to my Lord, to have the new
          King come to him; I must tell him, he is entring.
          O Heaven help, help;

*Enter* Lysip. Melant. Cal. Cleon, Diph. Strato.

*Lys.*    Where's *Amintor*?

*Strat.*  O there, there.

*Lys.*    How strange is this!

*Cal.*    What should we do here?

*Mel.*    These deaths are such acquainted things with me,
          That yet my heart dissolves not. May I stand
          Stiff here for ever; eyes, call up your tears;
          This is *Amintor*: heart he was my friend;
          Melt, now it flows; *Amintor*, give a word
          To call me to thee.

*Amint.*  Oh!

*Mel.*    *Melantius* calls his friend *Amintor*; Oh thy arms
          Are kinder to me than thy tongue;
          Speak, speak.

*Amint.*  What?

*Mel.*    That little word was worth all the sounds
          That ever I shall hear agen.

*Diph.*   O brother! here lies your Sister slain;
          You lose your self in sorrow there.

*Mel.*    Why *Diphilus*, it is
          A thing to laugh at in respect of this;
          Here was my Sister, Father, Brother, Son;
          All that I had; speak once again;
          What youth lies slain there by thee?

*Amint.*  'Tis *Aspatia*.
          My senses fade, let me give up my soul
          Into thy bosom.

*Cal.*    What's that? what's that? *Aspatia!*

*Mel.*    I never did repent the greatness of my heart till now;
          It will not burst at need.

*Cal.*    My daughter dead here too! and you have all fine new tricks
          to grieve; but I ne're knew any but direct crying.

*Mel.*    I am a pratler, but no more.

*Diph.*    Hold Brother.

*Lysip.*    Stop him.

*Diph.*    Fie; how unmanly was this offer in you!
    Does this become our strain?

*Cal.*    I know not what the mat[t]er is, but I am
    Grown very kind, and am friends with you;
    You have given me that among you will kill me
    Quickly; but I'le go home, and live as long as I can.

*Mel.*    His spirit is but poor that can be kept
    From death for want of weapons.
    Is not my hand a weapon good enough
    To stop my breath? or if you tie down those,
    I vow *Amintor* I will never eat,
    Or drink, or sleep, or have to do with that
    That may preserve life; this I swear to keep.

*Lysip.*    Look to him tho', and bear those bodies in.
    May this a fair example be to me,
    To rule with temper: for on lustful Kings
    Unlookt for sudden deaths from heaven are sent!
    But curst is he that is their instrument.

Lightning Source UK Ltd.
Milton Keynes UK
01 February 2011

166728UK00001B/101/P